Black Lightning

Naomi's Dream

Jo Hammers
Paranormal Crossroads & Publishing

Black Lightning, Naomi's Dream

Cover Art by Jo Hammers, 2011.

Table of Contents

Black Lightning

Naomi's Dream

Jo Hammers

Paranormal Crossroads & Publishing

PREFACE

Naomi Toombs, a farm wife, discovers that her Amish husband, who wanders off and returns not knowing where he has been, has seven secret wives. Her husband's last and final attempt at wandering off, pretending to be Schizophrenic, causes the death of her two children. He pushes her down and then kicks her pregnant belly till she loses the seven month old daughter she is carrying. Her other child dies from exposure to the elements, running and trying to get help for her. Not being able to handle the nightmare loss of her children, she leaves her Amish community and starts over in the land of the English after her husband had been missing for five years. Twists and turns in the story lead her to the discovery that her husband is a polygamist and her new best friend in the land of the English is also married to him as well as the sister of a man she meets and falls in love with. Secret wives keep popping up.

CHAPTER ONE

Naomi's Dream

Naomi could feel Jack's warm body laying up against hers in the dark. It was such a pleasant feeling to have someone to cling to and not be in fear of Joel killing her as she slept. "I love you, Jack." She whispered. He did not answer. She snuggled into the warmth of his body, still half asleep. The previous night was the first time she had ever had a man seriously make love to her and make her feel like a woman. Her body had been just a convenience to her husband Joel. He had never made love to her. In one night's time, Jack had taught her the difference. Jack had made her one happy woman before he satisfied himself. She had never experienced that before.

She now understood what Molly had inferred when she stated that her father-in-law was one hell of a great lover. Jack, in her thinking, was divine in the bed. She was glad that Karen had discarded him. Then, a little confused, she asked herself when did Karen discard him? Her thinking seemed to be a little muddled. Jack was Karen's boyfriend.

Discarding her questions concerning Karen, Naomi wandered in thought back to a romantic evening when she had sat in a porch swing with Joel over eleven years before. She remembered leaning on his shoulder and fantasizing about the perfect Amish marriage and the twelve perfect children they would have after they were married the next day. Her naive dream lasted for three weeks. Joel then started pulling his two and three days disappearing acts. Now, she knew that he had met and married Karen three to five weeks after he had married her. Her Amish dream had died a slow, horrendous death.

On the evening that she had sat in the porch swing dreaming with him, she recalled how an extremely large, orange butterfly had flown about them, eventually landing on his shoulder. He had commented about a small cousin of his named Sarah that was fascinated with Monarch Butterflies. It was small talk, but she remembered every word of him telling her about his four year old cousin and how he thought she would wander away from the community one day, chasing butterflies. She remembered him inferring that Sara was like him and would one day probably take flight to worlds unknown on wings that no one saw. At the time she had not understood what he meant and had ignored the statement. It had been the eve of their wedding and she did not recognize the wanderlust in him. In her grief and having been shunned after her children's deaths, she had lost track of those in her Amish world like little Sarah who would be possibly sixteen or seventeen now. She wondered if Joel's butterfly cousin had remained in the community or flew away like Joel. They were cousins and did share the same genes. Maybe Joel had recognized his wanderlust in her.

Naomi was what the English called a mail order bride. A marriage between her and Joel had been arranged by the brethren. She was an orphan in a northern settlement who had finished her eighth grade education and needed a home. She was two days from her sixteenth birthday when she stepped off the bus as a mail order bride with one of the northern brethren accompanying her. Joel's parents couldn't find a bride for Joel in their own settlement, due to his reputation of killing small animals when he was a kid and trying to look up the dresses of some of the girls when he was in the seventh and eighth grade. Naomi and the brethren of the northern settlement had not been presented with that information. Naomi just remembered stepping off of the bus for the first time and seeing Joel's grinning face. He was the handsomest boy she had ever seen and instantly had a wildly beating, heart crush on him. Now, she knew there was a difference between attraction and knowing the love of a man who stood by you. Joel had not wanted her. What he wanted was to be out of his parent's house. She represented freedom from his parents to him and nothing more. He had put on a good smiling face till he was married to her, had the deed to twenty acres of his parent's land, and the brethren had held a 'Barn Raising' and had framed them a farm house. Then he started pulling his crazy spells and wandered in and out of her life.

Naomi rolled away from the warmth of Jack's back feeling the need to get up and go to the rest room. As she rolled over, she felt something suddenly poking her in the ribs. Feeling beneath the covers she pulled out a flashlight and then quickly turned over in fright and shock. Jack was not there. She rubbed her eyes in disbelief. She wasn't in Jack's bed. In the dark, she could see that she was on her pallet in her closet in her tiny third floor apartment. She had been asleep and dreaming she was in bed with Jack. Her first night of forever, or wedding night, and the cat fight with Marcus's married lover had all been a dream. Naomi burst into tears realizing that she was fully dressed and had just returned from the attorney's office. She remembered that she had entered her closet after her appointment and lay down on the pallet to think. She must have fallen asleep. A spare pillow was on the pallet next to her. In her sleep, she must have thought it was Jack. The most wonderful night of her life had been a dream. A tear rolled down her face. She wanted to return to the dream and Jack's arms and was extremely mad at herself for waking up.

As she sat there in tears, Naomi recalled the two odd angels in her dream. One was black and really big with a southern, snippy twang to her voice. The other was a young, white angel who wore glasses and grinned like a cat. The big black angel had turquoise wings and the young one had purple wings. Naomi was in shock. Colors were prideful in her Amish community. The two angels were flamboyant and mouthed each other. She did not know what to make of it. However, she knew they were real because angels only visited you in your sleep.

With tears running down her cheeks, Naomi thought of her passionate night of making love to Jack in her sleep. It had been wonderful and he had made her feel like a woman. It had been six years since she had slept with Joel and he had used her body. Sleeping with Joel and Jack were different. Jack did not use her body just to satisfy his physical needs. He had made love to her and made her feel like a woman. His arms and body had been everything she always thought a man's could be. She had sinfully enjoyed his gentle hands all over her and his kisses that were not just on her mouth. Naomi blushed. She had committed the sin of adultery in her sleep, willingly. She was ashamed of her sleeping sin, but at the same time was one happy woman. Jack had been a gentle, pleasant lover putting her needs first. Joel had used her body to satisfy himself, but he had never made love to her. In her sleep, Jack had taught her what making love making was and she had been very pleased with his touch.

Wiping the tears from her cheeks with her bare hands, Naomi thought once more about the two angels in the farmer's market portion of her dream. They were not nice to each other. The huge, black one with turquoise wings had threatened the wimpy teen one with purple wings. She had jerked the little angel up and told her she was going to curse her with pimples for lying. Naomi had always thought of angels as being holy, dressed in white robes, having white wings, and singing songs of praise to God or delivering messages from him to Earth. The two angels she saw definitely did not fit any of her imagining of how angels were to look or act. Perhaps God had sent her English angels and not Amish ones. She would have to give the subject some serious thought. Both angels were wearing nail polish as well as toenail polish and the big one looked really familiar.

Naomi was at a loss as to what her dream meant, other than in Jack's arms she had found love, pleasure, and safety. She longed to go back to her dream of 'HER FIRST NIGHT OF FOREVER' with Jack and not wake up. Now awake, she had to face reality and its seeming never ending loneliness. Now, she had to unlock her closet door, face her lonely world, and put in her year of silence waiting for justice for her children. She wondered, as she unlocked the three barrel latches, if God would hold her dream against her. She had truly found personal pleasure in her dream; adulterous sinning with Jack. Biting her lip, she also knew that she would now blush every time she looked at her friend, Jack. However, she also knew that she needed the dream memory, of making love to Jack, to have something to hold on to. Before the dream, she had felt as if she was in a huge body of water, no shore line in sight, was tired of swimming, and had nothing to grab hold of to keep herself a float. A memory of a dream lover's arms was better than no arms to hold you. She would now run in her mind to the dream and Jack's arms when she needed to escape from her seemingly never ending loneliness and nightmares.

Before leaving the dark closet, where she had fallen asleep and dreamed of forever, Naomi closed her eyes and asked God a question. Tears rolled down her cheeks as she did so.

"I saw your mouthy, colorful, strangely different angels in my sleep. I know you are hearing me or you would not have sent them to me. What I wish to know is the meaning of their visitation to me? Also, I wish to know why you let me experience love and a wedding night with Jack, when it is Marcus that I have serious feelings for?"

In the invisible, Frankie Frances stood with Osceola in the corner of the dark closet listening to Naomi's prayer.

"She is crying again. Why?" Frankie Frances asked. "Marcus loves her and wants to be with her if she would lighten up and give him a chance. Why would God let her make love to Jack and see us? We now have two more sets of dirty wings to send to Heaven's dry cleaners. I wish the white caps would let us just be us. We are just like them, only holier." Frankie Frances stated pulling a halo from her school uniform pocket and placing it crooked on her head while grinning like a Cheshire cat.

Halos and wings were accessories the angels wore when appearing only to humans. They were like costume jewelry. They adorned themselves with them, when needed, just as human women put on jewelry, scarves, or belts to complete their fashion statements.

"I gave her the dream, Frankie Frances. She needed something to hold on to, something to fantasize about. Marcus is about to pull the unthinkable in her book, and her love for him will die. Up to this point, he is all she has had to fantasize about and hang on to. I let her spend a night in a good man's arms and feel like a woman. She will hold on to that. You will understand when you are older."

"What about us? Why did we step into her dream where she could see us? We are real angels, not dream scene visitors. I just was not in the mood to have to wear wings today. My allergies are acting up and the feathers just about did me in." Frankie Frances stated suddenly sneezing and her nose starting to drip.

"Naomi needs to know that her God's angels are watching over her." Osceola replied as Naomi rose and left her closet.

"Humans are always seeking a sign, or an angel visitation. I am a guardian angel, not an exhibitionist."

"Your hiding beneath her card table was not exactly the appropriate, visitation appearance of a guardian angel. The next time I take you into the dream world, please don't tremble in fear and hide when things get out of control. It is Earth humans that are suppose to tremble and hide their face from us. Naomi should have been under the table, not you!" Osceola stated in her syrupy, sticky, fly swatting voice as she rolled her eyes in disgust at her assistant.

"I wasn't hiding, I was taking a nap. Furthermore, I just don't see what is so important about Naomi having a fantasy about sleeping in the arms of her friend Jack. He is not nearly as nice looking as Marcus. In my book, Jack is ordinary at best. Why would anyone want to fantasize about ordinary or a man who runs around in khaki shorts, an island wildly colored floral shirt, and a panama straw hat? Marcus dresses in mall clothing suitable for his social position as a college professor. Have you ever looked at him from behind? He looks good in his tight fitting, designer jeans."

Jack's dream is to live in the islands somewhere. He is not ordinary or poorly dressed. He is dressing for success. In his book, success is living in the islands and having a gorgeous island girl on his arm and a houseful of exotic kids that he combs the beaches with. Success is different to each human. He is dressing for his success and will achieve his island goal. Jack is far from being ordinary. Marcus, on the other hand, is hiding in his designer jeans. Expensive clothing and a house in the suburbs to him is a sign of respectability. Respectability comes from within, not the clothing we wear. Marcus is basically a hooker the same as his sister in Nashville. He now tries to hide his fornications behind his designer jeans, house, and his teaching credentials. He would like to destroy or hide how he achieved his success, now that he has met Naomi. Success is not a pleasant experience if you have achieved it in ways you cannot speak of. Jack has stories to tell of his life as a police officer and then a detective to his someday children and the woman he will marry. Marcus wears a false face of respectability and tries to hide how he got where he is. Jack is a good man and capable of loving one special woman like Naomi for a lifetime. Marcus is too busy trying to hide his past and clinging to his sister and nephew's darkness to choose and love one respectable woman like Naomi and forsake all others. She is everything Marcus wants and has not achieved. He wears a false face of respectability. She and Jack wear the real thing. You will understand when you are a woman someday. Naomi needs a good man to fantasize about, not a false face.

"You treat me like I am a kid. I am a woman and am almost fourteen. I know what it is like to have someone special to fantasize about. I once met this really cute boy at the county fair. He was a vendor who sold pink cotton candy. After the fair, he and the carnival moved on. I would think about him and see him in my day dreams giving me a special, extra large, cone of his pink fluff. In my fantasy, I would take the cotton candy and put it on my head making a pink, spun candy wig. In my fantasy, pink hair was the in thing and it made me prettier, and more socially acceptable than any of my school friends or the cheerleaders. All the girls wanted to be me. The vendor boy, I never knew his name, would hitchhike back to me and all the girls would drool over him. They would all watch as he nibbled cotton candy from around my ear. I was cotton candy delicious and he couldn't resist me. See . . . I know about day dream fantasies and that loving feeling you get from a man's touch. His nibble tickled like a bug walking across your arm unexpectedly. I had to swat him off of my ear a few times."

"I suppose, you are going to give cotton candy dreams to the women you are assigned to someday when you get your guardian angel status?" Osceola Black Lightning asked rolling her eyes. "Arms, Frankie Frances, a grown woman wants to be held in a man's arms, not be a sugar high for some bug eyed, ear nibbler."

"We have differing opinions." Frankie Frances replied in her honey dipped voice. "You do your angel job your way, and I will do mine the way I want. Let me give Naomi a cotton candy dream next and we will see which she prefers. Of course, you will have to loan me your nail file sword. I seem to recall you destroying mine." She retorted in a syrupy, sticky, honey dipped face slapping voice.

"Touch my nail file, and you will be laid to rest in a coffin filled with pink cotton candy. Then you can experience the tiny mouths of maggots nibbling the pink stuff from your ears."

"And what has got you in such a foul mood this morning? I am always trying to be nice to you and trying to give you good advice. You are a narrow minded, over the hill death angel who has forgotten what it is like to have fun. Cotton Candy is fun. Naomi needs some fun in her life. We should have it for our meal, later. You definitely are lacking sugar in your disposition. If you had been more cotton candy fun, your long legged Jack Rabbit would now be holding onto your skirt tail instead of a fishing pole up north. I bet he has traded you in for some waitress there who knows how to be cotton candy to a man, if the truth were known. Pink sweet, you are not." Frankie Frances stated in her sticky, slapping young voice.

"I am a fine dining, lobster, steak, and escargot girl. I don't dine on pink tinted, spun sugar; nor do I date men who snack on crap candy. I am shrimp, steak, and fine dining to my long legged Jack Rabbit man. If you would eat less sugar crap, your pimples would probably clear up and you could attract a hamburger and french-fry man instead of a nibbling worm." Osceola retorted in her sticky, syrupy, fly swatting voice.

"There you go picking on me again. What have I done this morning to deserve your uncalled for, verbal attack? I am going to tell the White Suit on you when we get home. He likes me and you will be in deep dog doo-die when he finds out you have not been nice to me. Just so you know, I have been thinking about asking to move in with God and Mrs. God. They have plenty of room and stuffy angel dorms are not for me. The White Suit's palace is my style. I am a cotton candy, golden four poster bed sleeping, eat at the royal table girl. When you bow at their feet, I will be sitting on a little throne next to them and you will be also bowing at my feet."

Osceola began to belly laugh. Although she found her assistant to be totally intolerable, she had to give her credit. She had guts. Also, she wanted to be there when Frankie Frances asked the White Suit to move in with him. He had just pawned the teen disaster off on her. She definitely wanted to hear his reply.

CHAPTER TWO

Marcus Disappears

Saturday once more rolled around and Naomi made her way to the farmer's market. Her dream of Jack making love to her and the cat fight was still vivid in her mind. Naomi was sure she would blush every time she now looked at her friend Jack at the market. However, she was not willing to forget about the love she had experienced in Jack's bed and arms in the dream. It had helped to get her thru her lonely week. Even so, she was looking forward to seeing Marcus. She knew that she was going to have to cool her friendship with him to please Dan Maynard. However, that did not erase the feelings she had for him.

Surprisingly, Marcus was not at the market, nor was her folding table set up for her. Naomi was disappointed not getting to see him, but at the same time saw it as an opportunity to break in a new vendor booth spot across the aisle. Not having a table, she set up her display on the ground on her red checked table cloth. She glanced at Jack setting up his display across the aisle next to where Marcus usually set up. When he turned and gave her a little wave, she blushed but gave a little wave back and then looked him over really good, when he was not looking her way. He was very interesting looking in his khakis, floral island shirt, and panama straw hat. She wondered why she hadn't ever noticed how nice looking he was before. Suddenly, in her mind, he was standing there in the nude like he had been in her dream sleeping with her. She bit her lip and quickly turned her face from him. Lusting after someone other than Marcus had not been a problem till now. It was going to take months of Bible reading and prayer to get rid of her sudden lust for Jack. She knew she wanted more of him and that was wrong.

After Jack got his display set up, he walked across the aisle with a thermos of coffee offering her a cup.

"What is up Sweet Thing? Is there a reason for you setting up your display over here and where is Marcus?" He asked pouring her some coffee in a spare cup he had.

"Dan Maynard says I am to have no male friends for the next year. The tattoo man in St. Louis is Joel and I am in a year of waiting to go to court. I am thankful Marcus is not here this morning. It has given me the chance to choose a new spot. Where he is, I do not know."

"I understand!" Jack replied sipping his cup of coffee. "If I come to your apartment for any reason, I will make sure that Karen or someone female is with me."

"You always do what is right for me. I appreciate that about you and might I say I like your island shirt this morning. You look fun."

Jack grinned at her. "I am saving my money, Naomi. Someday when I retire, I am going to fly to an island somewhere and live out my life as a beach bum. I am going to find myself the prettiest island girl, marry her, and have a hut full of little Jacks. For now, my look is what keeps me going."

"I will miss you someday. I hope your island girl will understand that you are my friend and belong a thimble size full to me." She replied reaching up with a finger on her free hand and wiping what looked like a doughnut smudge from the right corner of his mouth. He was like her Adam. She couldn't resist touching him up sometimes. He always had a crooked tie or something needing her attention.

Jack held his coffee cup steady in one hand while she wiped the corner of his mouth. Her touch was gentle and it sent shivers down him. She was everything he had ever dreamed about having in a woman. He could see himself living in the islands with her and having a slew of little girls in gray dresses just like her trailing along behind them making foot prints in his island's sand. To him, an island girl wasn't some native in a grass skirt and skimpy bikini top. An island girl to him was the perfect woman with her arm linked in his walking on the beach with him and them growing old and dying in each other's arms. The right woman to love him and wipe doughnut smudges from his face was paradise. Naomi was who he wanted to spend paradise and eternity with. She was slowly turning from her feelings for Marcus. He was a patient man. Once his arms held her, he was never letting her go. Marcus was a fool. This was the third Saturday he had not been at the market and he knew why.

"I must be careful according to my attorney." Naomi stated pausing to take a sip of her cup of coffee. "My in-laws are very wealthy Amis farmers and might pay for Joel's defense. Dan Maynard says they may even go so far as to have a detective follow me for the next year. If I divorce Joel and prove my case of polygamy, their son will be shunned back home. If my in-laws want to remain Amish, they would have to shun Joel also. My attorney says they will probably do everything possible to keep Joel from being shunned. His mother is a vindictive woman who got me shunned for no reason. Joel is my mother-in-law's favorite son. She will see me and my accusations as an open declaration of war on her, not Joel. I must be very careful, even about being seen standing too close to you. I should not have wiped the doughnut from your mouth just now. That could have been photographed and stretched to mean something it was not."

"I understand, Naomi. On Thursdays, I will not come to your apartment to get my tie straightened till this is all over. I will tighten my relationship with Karen so that you have no reason to worry about our friendship being a problem. However, you always remember that you and I are family. I will never forget what you did for me last winter and I will be lurking in the shadows if you need me. I understand your need to get a divorce and get Joel out of your life."

"Mr. Maynard says blood is thicker than water. He says my in-laws will turn on me, even though Joel is in the wrong. Also, he pointed out to me that Marcus will stand by his sister and not me when the chips are down, as he puts it. If my children were alive, I would stand by them till Hell froze over, no matter what. My blood is thicker than water."

"Well, Sweet Thing, in case you have forgotten, you gave me a pint of your blood when I was in need in the hospital. We have the same blood flowing thru our veins. I will stand by you, till hell freezes over."

Naomi grinned. "I had forgotten that. I am you and you are me."

"Our blood is forever joined in the sight of your God. You have a guarantee that I will always stand by you. My allegiance is to you. You proved to me last winter your allegiance, as well as became the only family I have. This island loving boy has your back."

"I trust you, Jack. Now, I know why. We are of the same blood." She stated finishing her cup of coffee and handing him his cup. "Oh, I forgot. You might as well eat Marcus' fritter. Apparently, he has abandoned us for some reason." She stated handing him an apple fritter which he took with a happy expression on his face.

Jack sniffed the apple fritter and then took a bite thinking that his old friend Marcus was losing ground.

"Karen and I are taking a walk down by the river tonight. Would you like to join us? You could walk on the other side of Karen."

"Karen is one very lucky lady. I will let her be one lucky lady and enjoy your arm alone." Naomi replied looking him over. She had never really paid too much attention as to how he looked, till now. She blushed looking at his khaki pants, the colorful island shirt he wore with parrots all over it, and his panama hat with a colorful hat band. He had explained to her last winter ,that he one day wanted to live in the islands, marry an island girl, and have at least six little beach bums and bunnies to share his retirement world. Naomi blushed while watching him eat his fritter. He was a man, a very delicious looking man. Since her dream, she could see him without his clothes on in her mind. She bit her lip.

"You are blushing. Do you want to tell me what that is all about?" He asked pouring her some more coffee from his thermos.

"Hot flashes . . ." She replied quickly needing to come up with a quick explanation. "I am not young and I am having a problem right now. I have an early onset." Then she really blushed. Amish women didn't discuss that sort of thing out in public, much less with a man.

"I am not getting any younger myself." He laughed. "Where is Marcus this morning?" He asked pointing to the empty vendor stall.

"I do not know. Perhaps he is spending the morning with his married lady friend. Wherever he is at, he has my card table."

"I can fix that. After we drink our coffee, I will borrow four milk crates from the snack shack girl and a board which I will lay across them making you a table. If Marcus doesn't return with your table next week, I will loan you an old one I have in my apartment as well as a padlock and key. You can chain it to your post like some of the other regular vendors do."

"Thank You! You are a true friend, Jack." She stated pausing before asking a question she wanted an answer for. "I have a question to ask you."

"If you are asking me to marry you after your divorce, you will have to take it up with Karen. She seems to be making all of my important decisions now-a-days." He stated to throw her off guard. As long as she thought he was serious about Karen, she would let him wander in and out of her life and apartment like a brother. For now, that was his edge over Marcus. He could visit Naomi any time he wanted in her apartment as long as he had a woman on his arm. Plus, Karen was a safe date. She was still in love with her ex. There were no commitment issues.

"I might like a man that I could make all the decisions for. My first decision would be to put you in long pants. It is cool today. Aren't you cold in your island shorts?"

"Actually, I am. Do the goose bumps on my hairy legs show?" He asked teasing her.

"I would have demanded this morning that you put on long pants and a turtleneck beneath your island shirt. Your arms have goose bumps also."

"What about my cold nose?" He asked laughing as she redressed him in her mind. In all reality, he knew that he would wear anything she wanted him to, eat anything she wanted him to, and be anything she wanted him to. He just wanted her to love him forever.

"One of the ladies I clean for moved here from Alaska. She tells me that the Eskimos kiss by rubbing noses. Kisses make you very warm. If you were my man, I would now Eskimo kiss you over and over till your nose was warm. I will pass that tip on to Karen."

"What if I had a runny nose?" He smirked loving his interaction with her.

"I guess it would be like sharing my toothbrush, we would Eskimo kiss and then share a handkerchief. We probably would also share a head cold."

"It might be nice having a nose warmer. I will ask Karen if I can have you and her. What do you think she will say?" He asked laughing.

"I am sure she would tell you to take your cold nose and stick it somewhere. She uses that phrase quite often when she speaks of her ex. You just might suddenly find yourself as a second ex."

"Your point is taken. Since it is Karen that I am in love with," he stated lying. "I will have to do without your nose warmer. A man has to make choices."

"Karen is lucky to have you. I would like to have Marcus choose only me. May I ask you my question? We wandered away from my thought."

"Sure Sweet Thing. Ask me anything. If I know the answer I will give it to you."

"I know that you and Marcus have been lifetime friends. Do you think Marcus is rolling in the hay again with his married lover named Jenkins? My attorney informed me that Marcus is a user of married women. I am questioning his reason for friendship with me. Does he just want to one day roll in the hay with me seeing me as some sort of game?"

"Well, Sweet Thing. If he is once more sleeping with Jenkins, he is a fool. He is not the only one that she has been rolling in the hay with. He was in love with her and did ask her to divorce her husband and marry him. He wanted her to move to California with him. She turned him down just before you came wandering into the farmer's market last fall. I have to be honest with you. She is one damn, good looking woman. I understand why Marcus or any man, excluding me, would fall into her bed. She has everything going for her. She has looks, money, social connections, and just recently received her doctor's degree. She is the number ten that Marcus has spent his life trying to achieve. The only flaw in her, that Marcus doesn't see, is that she has a taste for men, not just one man. He is not a number ten to her. He is just one more male on her adulterous belt. Men fall into her bed and behind her husband's back."

"If you ever fall into her bed, I will put you over my knees and spank you. She is married and you know better. As you once told me, your mother was a Sunday school teacher. You know the laws of God."

"That I do, Sweet Thing. You don't have to worry about me falling in her bed. I see her for what she is, a high class whore. However, may I take a rain check on that spanking? I will go this week and find a married woman to roll in the hay with? Next Saturday night, you can lay one on my naked backside. I might like it."

"You are awful. I should spank you, just for wishing to be over my knees."

Jack laughed. "Everyone has their fetishes. Mine just might be being spanked by you."

"I should spank you just for thinking bad thoughts. However, I will restrain myself and only spank you for rolling in the hay with a married woman."

"Well, Naomi, I have been meaning to tell you, I slept with a married woman last Monday, another on Tuesday , six on Wednesday, another on Thursday , and five yesterday on Friday. Does that qualify me for bending over your knees tonight? My Sweet Thing named Naomi can beat my ass if she wants, before I take Karen out to dinner." He smirked.

"I should put you over my knees for lying. You have just had surgery and cannot handle fourteen married women in one week. You do not have the physical stamina. However, I have the stamina to swing my arm and discipline your backside good for lying. Because you have been ill, however, I am giving you a rain check and will lay it on you when you are fully recovered for lying."

"I will collect on that rain check when your divorce is over and my body has recuperated. Karen will just have to understand if I have a case of the red beaten butt."

"You are my friend and should not tease me. I am lonely and I just might enjoy spanking your bottom. It has been awhile since I took a good look at a man's bare butt."

"I should be so lucky . . . !" He laughed. Then he left her to her morning. He had a customer across the aisle.

"I should be so lucky . . . !" She muttered remembering how comforting it was to have his body next to hers in her dream and his hands all over her when he made love to her.

About an hour later, Marcus showed up at the market and quickly set up his display.

"You are messing with trouble again." Jack whispered helping him, so that Naomi wouldn't hear. He and Marcus had been friends for years. He recognized Jenkins perfume on his friend. "You reek with Jenkins perfume."

"Jenkins called and insisted I meet her for coffee at the truck stop this morning. Some detective is hounding her and she is afraid our affair is going to be found out by her husband. She thinks her husband might be having us followed. She wanted to come out here to the market and talk behind my booth. You can imagine how that would have gone over with Naomi. I am trying to keep my past affair with Jenkins hidden from Naomi."

"Sooner or later, you are going to have to tell Naomi about Jenkins and all the married women you slept with for money putting yourself thru college. You were a Gigolo; in case you have forgotten." Jack stated as he stacked gourds onto Marcus' table.

Jack had been Marcus's best friend in high school and college. Jack had graduated the University with a degree in law enforcement and related studies. Marcus chose Science and related studies. They had always done everything together except the gigolo bit. Jack had money to pay for his education.

"I don't plan to ever tell Naomi, if I can help it. I quit seeing Jenkins last fall when Naomi showed up at the market."

"Well, you sure reek with her perfume this morning." Jack retorted in a low voice. "You had to be pretty damn close to her for her scent to rub off on you."

"I do what I have to do, Jack, to survive. This morning it was meeting Jenkins at the truck stop to keep her from showing up here to talk. Naomi is the only woman I will ever love. I knew it the moment I saw her last fall. I need a little smooth sailing with Naomi and that means stuffing my past as far down into nowhere as I can get it. Plus, Jenkins doesn't know about Naomi. I wouldn't put it past her just walking up to Naomi's apartment door and telling her every detail of our three years in bed together as well as about the money she has given me over the years. Where is Naomi, anyway?"

Jack pointed across the aisle and down a little ways. "You weren't here, so she decided to try out a new spot. I made her a table out of some milk crates and a board."

"I suppose someone else has eaten my fritter too?" He stated angry looking at his watch. He had looked forward to spending the morning with her and his fritter.

"Actually, Marcus, I ate it. I shared my thermos of coffee with her and she gave me your fritter thinking you were not coming. Where have you been the last two Saturdays? Have you been with Jenkins or has your sister dumped her kids on you again?"

23

"My sister got thrown out of her apartment. She dumped the kids on me till she could rent another after sucking the money out of me for the new apartment. I took Adam and his two sisters home to her last Sunday. Day care for them here is really becoming a problem. Adam has been banned from most of them from his numerous stays with me. My neighbors won't even watch him for an hour. I have had to take him everywhere with me the last two weeks and that includes into my classroom. I couldn't bring him here with me the last couple of Saturdays. Adam called Naomi a bunch of foul names and was just overly rude to her for some reason. I brought him back to make him apologize three Saturdays ago, but she had already gone home. Is Adam the reason she has moved across the aisle?" He asked knowing the answer and also a little pissed over her telling him that Adam was a little heathen before he had taken Adam home in disgust.

"I am sure she has her reasons for moving across the aisle. If you and Adam are the reasons, then suck it up and live with it. Naomi is respectable. Face it, Marcus, Adam is a wild, mouthy, little gutter rat. Your sister has chosen to raise him to be that. He isn't domesticated or house broken."

"Adam will change when I adopt him someday." Marcus retorted angrily. "Adam is just a little kid who needs me."

"Your sister is a gutter whore and you are a high class gigolo. She is raising him to be a gutter rat and what do you have to offer him? Are you going to raise him to be a servicer of women like yourself to get what he wants out of life? Adam will one day grow up to walk on the shady side of life, just like you and Angela."

"I am respectable now and I will make Adam respectable too." Marcus shot back in a low voice that the other vendors could not hear. "Adam may have used foul language and called Naomi names a few Saturdays ago. However, that will change once I have custody of him and teach him some manners."

"Naomi is respectable, Marcus! Face it, your nephew is a little heathen. He has been raised in the gutter and displays all of its low class mannerisms. He is a low class gutter rat just like you are a high class one. A rat is a rat, and a rat can't teach a baby rat to be anything they are not. Your respectability has been paid for by your engaging in the illegal trade of male prostitution. You are a male whore. Naomi is not a gutter rat. She is respectable and what you have always said you wanted out of life. The way I see it, you are probably going to have to make a choice between a respectable life with Naomi' or a life in the gutter with your nephew. Naomi will never take your foul mouthed nephew into her home and arms, much less raise him."

"Why are you on my case this morning? I am doing the best I can do and you are wrong about Adam."

"We have always told each other the way it is. That is the reason we are friends. We don't pull any punches with each other. Normally, we trust each other's opinion. I am not telling you anything about yourself or your nephew that you don't already know."

"Adam and his sisters are my family, Jack. I just can't toss them aside like they are meaningless. There isn't a doubt in my mind that Angela will lose them soon. I won't see them being raised by strangers. Jenkins was my last money bag. I am making it fine now on my professor's wages and I will raise Adam and his sisters well and never tell them what my sister is or what I had to do to get my education. If I have to, I will move to California with them and Naomi where no one knows me."

"I have not known Naomi long, but she has become my friend just like you. She has earned my respect and allegiance. Last winter, she was there for me when I had no family to turn to."

"I assume you are referring to your surgery. You told me that she came to visit you while you were in the hospital."

"You and I have been friends for at least ten years or longer. You came to see me once. Naomi came every day, and walked in a heavy snow to do so."

"How long were you in the hospital?" Marcus asked.

"I was in there for ten days sick as a dog. Naomi stayed with me when I was at my worst, holding my hand, praying for me, and helping me on and off those damn bedpans. She bathed me, fed me, and handed me the damn urinals. I was basically a stranger to her, but she stood by me when she discovered that I was there in the hospital all alone. She was there for me as a friend when I was naked and at my worst. Now, she is at the top of my list when it comes to friends. There will be no foul mouthed Adams in my world disrespecting her, if they want to keep their teeth. You have your priorities all wrong, Marcus. If Naomi is the love of your life, as you have told me, she should come first and the adoption of your nephew forgotten about. In my opinion, he would be better off raised in a juvenile center where they know how to control his mouth and other mannerisms."

25

"My nephew is family, Jack. I will adopt him. Naomi will just have to live with it. I am rescuing Adam and his sisters when the time comes."

"Your adopting Adam is not going to be saving him, as you see it. I have a degree in law enforcement, in case you have forgotten. Your nephew is on the road to becoming a criminal just like your sister. You don't knowingly stuff a criminal into the arms of a woman you love. You protect her from the criminal."

Marcus thought about what Jack said. However, the only part of their conversation he heard was the part where he spoke of Naomi bathing and carrying for his naked body. He was pissed.

"Damn you Jack. I can't get Naomi to let me step inside her apartment door and you have her bathing your naked ass for two weeks. I am not pleased with that. You should have hired a private sitter to wash your sorry ass."

"It was longer than two weeks that Naomi was there for me. She came every day to my apartment for six weeks after I was out of the hospital to make sure my bandages were changed and that I was fed, shaved, and showered. She washed my back and everything else I have, when I couldn't. I owe her big time."

"She washed your . . . ?" Marcus sputtered turning green with jealousy.

"Yes, and every other inch of my ill body. I have a respect and feelings for Naomi that I have never had for any woman but her. If Naomi ever dumps you for any reason, I am going to put one of the biggest rocks on her finger that you ever saw and will be permanently eating your apple fritters. I have no Jenkins or hundreds of married lovers to have to explain to her or foul mouthed nephews to try to push off on her."

"You back off, Naomi is my girl." Marcus replied mad.

"You say she is your girl, I say she will one day be mine because you can't stay away from Jenkins and are unwilling to forget about Adam." Jack stated grinning, knowing he had his friend Marcus stewing in his own juices.

Marcus was pissed that his best friend was waiting in the wings to move in on him with Naomi. However, he did have to give Jack credit. He had been up front about it.

A couple of customers interrupted their conversation.

After his customer, Marcus returned to his thoughts. All winter he had planned reasons to get Naomi to walk down by the river or spend time with him after market hours. Adam had first ruined his river walking plans, Jenkins was trying to compound them, and now he had a serious rival for Naomi. How was he ever going to find a way out of his rat maze?

As Marcus was thinking about walking across the aisle and getting his apology over, concerning Adam, his cell phone rang. He immediately recognized his sister's phone number.

"What is up, Angela?" He asked roughly due to his pissed off mood. He had just taken the kids home to her and given her money five days prior. "I am at the market and I am busy! Did I forget something when I brought Adam and his sister home last night. I bought you diapers and formula for the baby. What do you want now? I am busy. Call one of your Nashville friends to gab."

"Well, get un-busy. I need you to come back and get this crying baby now! I have had all I can take! She is a little crying monster. I would like to cram my fist down her throat and then beat her head against the wall. If you don't come, I just might kill and dump this damn kid in the dumpster out back. She won't stop crying and I have had it with her. I broke open a sleep medicine capsule and gave that to her in some soda. That hasn't even stopped her crying. I have had it, Marcus. Joe has been gone for six months and I have had it. These kids are history. I just might take a butcher knife to all three of them."

"Don't do anything, foolish, Angela. Take the baby to a neighbor and just walk away. I will be there as quick as I can tomorrow morning. I can't come today. Take Adam and his sister to day care and don't go back to get them. I will come tomorrow morning, get the three, and pay any child care fees."

"You don't care! You are a piece of shit, Marcus! Maybe I should just take and drown them in the bath tub. It was Joe that wanted them and now he is gone. A nice little apartment fire might work. That would get Adam, Mary, and this crying baby monster out of my hair for good."

"I will leave now, Angela and be there as quick as I can. Take the baby to the neighbor and put Adam and Mary outside and let them play on the sidewalk." Marcus stated in alarm feeling the two would be safer on the street unwatched, than in an apartment that she might actually set on fire.

There was no reply on the other end of the line. All he could hear was the baby crying and his sister yelling obscenities at Adam and Mary and asking them what they had done with her cigarette lighter.

Marcus knew his sister had no common sense when she was out of control and was capable of doing anything. He had witnessed her strangling kittens in their barn, just for the heck of it, when they were just a year or so older than Adam was now. His sister hadn't killed a human yet, but he did not put it past her capabilities. He feared Adam and his two sisters would not live to see another day.

"I am leaving now." He yelled into the phone and then hung up.

Immediately, Marcus called the Nashville police department and repeated his sister's story about the adult sleeping med that Angela said she had given the baby. He did not repeat the apartment fire words. He wanted to get the baby into safe hands, not label his sister as a possible arsonist. He asked the police to send someone quick that the baby might be in serious trouble and that his sister's other two young children were probably running loose in the street. He was too far away to prevent any tragedy. He then jumped in his jeep, forgetting his need to apologize to Naomi, and left the market heading once more for Nashville to rescue Adam and his sisters.

As he drove, he thought of his parents who just lived across the Missouri line from Nashville. He was pissed that they didn't step up to the plate and take on some of the responsibility for Angela and their grandchildren. The baby, Adam, and Mary could be swept into the social service foster care program and they didn't give a damn. They had turned their back on their daughter.

Marcus returned his thoughts to his sister. This was the first time that she had threatened to murder one of her kids. He had to trust that the police would scoop up the baby and place her into foster care, as well as the other two. He was sure his sister had to be high on drugs. She sounded as though she were bouncing off the walls.

As he was driving, the Nashville police did call him back and tell him that they had entered the apartment and had found the baby convulsing. They told him that they were taking the baby to the emergency room and Adam and Mary was in the hands of his sister's new landlord till he got there. They also informed him that his sister was drunk as a skunk and had passed out with an empty bottle of vodka next to her chair. Marcus shook his head in disgust. His sister was white trash and he was tired of picking up the pieces of her life. She always picked the worst possible moments to pull her crap on him. He needed to concentrate on making up with Naomi, not having to dash off to Nashville to pick up a newborn and two small kids that he was not prepared to handle. He called Angela's landlord and explained he would be there in two hours to get them and that he would pay her for her time. She seemed okay with it. She hadn't had time yet to know what Mary and Adam were like. Then he called the hospital emergency room and told them he was the guardian of the baby and he was on the way from out of state to get it and pay for any hospital bills in hopes that Social services didn't catch wind of the drug that the baby had been given. He lied and told the emergency room that the baby had a history of convulsions and was on a sleep medication. He didn't want to see his sister in jail for the murder of her own child. He prayed that the baby would survive the sleeping pill that he didn't have a clue what was.

As he drove, he was in a pissed mood. Angela just continually sucked the breath out of him and his finances. He needed money to buy Naomi an engagement ring to plop on her finger the day her divorce came thru. Jack was not moving in on him. If he had too, he would roll over with a few more married hags to get the money. Jack possibly making a play for Naomi totally annoyed him. Worse yet, he knew that Naomi needed him. It had been weeks since his discovery and he hadn't got a chance to approach the subject with her yet about her sleeping on the floor in a locked closet. He couldn't even touch that subject till he explained why Adam had a foul mouth and the fact that he did try to make Adam apologize to her before taking him back home to Nashville three weeks before. He wanted to be walking down by the river this afternoon with Naomi, not sitting in a jeep in stalled traffic trying to rescue his sister's kids in Nashville.

CHAPTER THREE

Karen's Story

A couple more Saturdays passed and Marcus did not return to the market. Naomi wondered what had happened to him. At the same time, she was glad she had the peace to get her newly located booth up and running without having to give any explanations. Jack had kept his word and provided her a card table and a small padlock and key. She did business as usual selling her breads and jellies. The only difference being, she was now settled into a new routine on the other side of the Farmer's Market aisle. Jack was also missing from the market on Saturdays. However, he had a legitimate excuse for doing so. He told Naomi he was working the biggest case of his whole career. However, he popped in on her during the week in the evenings when he was in town. He kept his word and never dropped in without Karen on his arm, for appearances sake.

On the nights Jack was home, he was of immense help to Naomi. He seemed to always sense what she was in need of. He regularly carried out her trash, swept her third floor landing, and washed the pots and pans for her as she baked breads for the market. Jack became her extra hands and seemed to be happy doing the remedial tasks. He even wore one of Naomi's aprons to protect the front of his dress khakis. The two girls teased him about it. He once retorted, "A smart man knows when to wear his woman's apron." Naomi had been very pleased with his comment. She was slowly seeing that he was everything a man should be. At the same time, she couldn't rid herself of her secret feelings for Marcus. She knew it should be Jack that her heart was racing for.

Karen was just as lonely as Naomi and joined in on the regular baking and wrapping of breads in the third floor tiny apartment. The three formed a bond of friendship. Only Naomi knew that it would end within a few months. Karen would turn on her when she discovered they shared the same sinful, woman chasing husband. Jack would have to give up their friendship if he wanted to continue dating Karen. Naomi tried not to think about losing Jack as her friend. She had grown quite attached to him, in spite of the fact that he was dating Karen. She took her world one day at a time and tried to make the most of it.

Naomi had one goal in mind, get justice for her children. If it meant laying her friends down, she would do it. Her children did not deserve to die.

Marcus had temporarily disappeared from their lives. Naomi was broken hearted about it, but was at the same time sure his intentions were not honorable toward her. Finding out that he was a male harlot had been a hard fact for her to swallow. She tried not to think about him rolling in the hay with one of his many married lovers. So, she clung to her fantasies about Jack to fill her lonely nights and Saturdays.

It was Saturday evening about seven. One more selling day at the Farmer's Market had been successful. Naomi had put her tote and items away, showered, and then prepared to spend the evening reading her Bible. Marcus and Jack had not been at the market. Beyond it, Naomi had no social life. She cleaned houses, prayed, baked bread, red her Bible, cried and then repeated the process. She missed her Saturdays with Marcus. For some reason, he had quit attending the market. Naomi just accepted the fact that their friendship had gone permanently sour. The last time she saw him, they had been at odds over his nephew Adam. She did regret that their friendship had ended in words over a child that was of no importance to her, other than he was a clue leading her to Joel. She half way wished that she could go back to the days at the market before Adam. Although blind to who Marcus really was, the times they had shared were happy ones. Happy moments were few and far between now in her life.

A knock sounded on Naomi's third floor door. Naomi cautiously opened it and peeped out. With her divorce growing closer, she feared that Joel would somehow find her and kill her. She was relieved to see that it was her landlord, Karen. She quickly wiped tears from her eyes. She had been crying over Marcus just before opening the door. She did not want to have feelings for a gigolo, but she did.

"Are you doing anything this evening?" Karen asked. "Jack and his camera are off and gone again. He tells me he is working the biggest case of his career. I swear he loves his camera more than me. Joey had a prostitute mistress and Jack's is his job and camera."

"The one thing I am not, is busy." Naomi replied stepping out on to the landing. "Do you have something in mind?"

"It is such a pretty evening. I thought we might walk downtown, look in some shop windows, wander down to the river, sit on a bench near the mural wall, and just have some girl talk. Are you interested? Between Joey and Jack abandoning me, I am a little depressed. My monthly is compounding my blues. I need someone to talk to."

"I understand that. My friendship with Marcus has bellied up and I am not very happy either. He has been gone from the market for four or five Saturdays now. I think he is rolling in the hay with his married lover again. I found out about her by accident."

"I hoped you would not get serious about him. He does have a shady side. It is a good thing that you know about her. If things had progressed between you and him, I knew that I was going to have to gossip and tell you about his long running love affair with the aunt of my friend Mavis."

"It is okay. I do not need a man to complicate my life right now. Lady friends are safe. When your cake is rising in the oven, they will not stomp across your floor making it fall." Naomi stated leaning against the third floor railing as was Karen who didn't seem to be in any hurry to start their walk.

"One time when Joey and I were first married back in Missouri, I grilled a couple of cheese sandwiches on some sour dough bread for lunch. I was on my lunch hour and I had to fix something that was quick. He sat down at the table, took one look at his grilled cheese sandwich and pushed it back informing me that he didn't eat cheap ass cheese sandwiches. I was so mad; I picked his plate up, walked over to the trash can, and dumped his in it. Then I took my sandwich and went back to work. He dared to ask me, as I was going out the door, what he was going to have for lunch. It was my monthly time and my emotions were a little strung out and in overdrive. I turned around and told him to go elsewhere and find him a woman who was willing to make him something besides a cheap ass cheese sandwich because it would not be me. I went into a rage and told him to leave and never come back that I was tired of his coming and going in my life and his picky eating habits. We were living with Aunt Molly at that time. He had no choice but to leave. Aunt Molly came out of the back room pointing a handgun when she heard us into it. She put a dead on single shot between his legs into the hardwood floor. She had him dancing and heading for the door. I heard nothing from him for six months and I didn't go looking for him. Aunt Molly and I are alike. We don't chase after discarded ass holes, we move on."

Naomi recalled a six month period when she was first married where Joel had not wandered off. They had a few months that were fairly happy, or at least she thought they were.

"When did he return to you?"

"He returned after getting wind that I was suing him for a divorce. I started college after he was gone and met a male music major student at the university and we hit it off. I left Joel a note on the convenience store bulletin board, where I first met him, telling him that I was suing him for a divorce and for him to contact my attorney. The gas station convenience store on state highway thirteen was where I picked him up and dropped him off for his trucking job. We also met there."

"Truck drivers do come and go. I can see where you were possibly tired of his wanderings in and out." Naomi replied knowing that the gas station was only about three miles from her and Joel's farm, if you cut across neighbor's fields. When he was suppose to be out on the road driving a truck in Karen's world, he had just walked back home across the fields to her.

"Joey's trucking schedule was so unpredictable. He would call saying he had just gotten off a truck and I would go pick him up at the gas station. The lot lizard he is now with and has children by, probably met him at some truck stop somewhere in Missouri. I do know she is from Missouri. I just don't know where."

"Why did you let him come back? You said you are like your Aunt Molly and dump your unwanted men."

"I didn't intend to. During his six month's absence, I met this wealthy, good looking, music major at the university. He was from here in Paducah. We were getting serious about each other and he was just about to take me home for a weekend to meet his parents. He was focused on becoming a teacher the same as me. Looking back, I can see that we were right for each other. Suddenly, Joey came waltzing back in after six months begging me not to divorce him spouting the sanctity of marriage. He broke up my new relationship by declaring his undying love for me. Like a fool, I took him back. My university guy moved on to someone else. As soon as Joey was sure that the guy I was seeing was history, he took up his old habits of wandering in and out as a truck driver again. He would drive a week or so out on the road and then out of the blue, pop back in. Sometimes his runs would be short and he would be gone a week or a few days. I should have divorced him and saved myself years of misery and loneliness."

"What happened to your university student friend?"

"He now has his doctorate and heads the music department at the university where he works. I could be living in the big house his wife now takes for granted here in Paducah. Instead, I spend my time living and surviving in a bottle wondering what Joey's next betrayal will be."

Naomi cringed on the inside. Joel had disappeared on her over and over for two or three days, or a week here and there. She now knew that he was running back and forth between her and Karen. He pretended he had mental madness to her and a truck driver to Karen.

"What happened after you took him back and broke up with your teacher friend?" Naomi asked fishing for more details.

"After being home for six months, Joey got a traveling salesman job which was as bad as being a truck driver. He then would be home a couple days and then sometimes be gone for two or three weeks. Sometimes, he would hit town with only a few hours to spare. We would go out to eat, make love in the middle of the day, and then he would be off and gone again. I was busy going to college and holding down a full time job. Joey never seemed to be around when our bills came due. He said he was saving his checks to put as a down payment on a house. I was stupid enough to believe him and paid all of our bills out of my wages. After he moved back in, much to the dismay of my aunt Molly, he took up with the Missouri prostitute behind my back. I don't know just when or where he met her or how they ended up in Nashville. All I know is that she is from Missouri and has three kids now by him, all born within the last six or so years. She was pregnant when he came to Paducah with a roll of cash asking me to take him back a second time. I threw him out a second time in my junior year of college and after graduation moved here alone to

Paducah, secretly hoping I could renew my relationship with my music major."

"You did not know about his pregnant harlot or her later kids?"

"I didn't have a clue till a year or so ago when I walked in on him and her down in Nashville. Afterward, I hired a detective to check her out. He informed me that she was pregnant with her oldest boy about the same time I had first moved here to Paducah. Joey and I had split up during my senior year of college and my first year here. I had a good new life started for myself. I had a teaching position, an apartment downtown, and a respectable new life for myself. I had just started dating Dan Maynard, the attorney. We had been out twice and a relationship between us looked promising. That was when Joey found me and came wandering back in and out of my life again."

Naomi thought of the two wonderful years she had with Joel that he had stayed home sane. Mary was their love child. It was the years Karen had thrown him out a second time. When he kicked her and left her on the floor giving birth and at the point of death, he was heading out for good to be with Karen. She and her children had meant nothing to Joel. It was Karen that he had loved and kept trying to return to. She would not have ever been accepted in the Amish community and that is why he held on to her till he was older and made the conscious decision that it was Karen he wanted; not his parents, her, or his Amish community.

"So, Joey was not in your life your senior year of college or your first year here?"

"No, I told him to take a hike after my junior year. I was maturing and deciding what I wanted out of live. I was crazy about him, but I could see that our worlds were just not compatible. I wanted what he wasn't willing to give me. I wanted a man with a steady pay check who was lying next to me every morning, not a sporadic jump, run, and disappear for days man. I watched my college and high school friends settling into the suburbs in Missouri and Kentucky with families and mortgages, and, and with goals for their retirement someday. Joey had no goals. He was a traveling sales man who never brought home a pay check and I was lucky for him to be in my bed three or four nights a month."

"I understand and agree. A man who loves you does not wander from your bed or fails to support you financially. The Bible says a man who does not provide for his household is worse than an infidel."

"He was definitely worse than an infidel. I rarely saw a dime of his pay-checks. If anything, I supported him and probably his whore in Nashville. It wasn't unusual for money to come up missing from my purse or my savings."

"He stole from you?" Naomi asked knowing that Joel had walked away from their marriage taking all of the crop money with no concern for how she would feed her two children or pay for medical care for her sick Adam.

"It seemed with each year of our life together, he was changing and not for the better. His thefts from me were nothing in comparison to his overall changes. He was a very handsome man with dark wavy hair and a beard. About the end of my junior year of college, he shaved his head. I was working and going to college and had very little free time to do housework. I came home and found him on my couch asleep and my bathroom sink full of his hair that he had not cleaned up. I was pissed and flew into a rage because of the hair in my sink and the fact that he looked like a criminal with his hair shaved off. We got into it and I told him to clean up his mess in the bathroom and that I was not going to be seen publicly with him till his hair grew back out. He told me that it wasn't a woman's place to tell the man what he could or couldn't do, that it was a woman's place to do as the man said. Naturally, the Aunt Molly in me came out. I peppered the lawn with his few clothes and called the police when he started to get physical with me. He slapped me hard just as the police arrived."

"Did they take him to Jail?" Naomi asked biting her lip and trying to control her own emotions and tears.

"The police threatened to shock him with their little electric cattle prods and haul him off to jail for assault. He backed off and left. I yelled after him that I never wanted to see him again and that I was suing him for a divorce. His slap caused me a dental problem and bill that zapped my finances at the time. I did not have the money to carry out my threat. He was gone, so I just ignored the divorce, telling myself I would get it as soon as I was out of my senior year and had my first real job and had money. When I got my first teaching posi-tion a year later, I did try to sue him for a divorce. The process server could not find him. He had just disappeared. The trucking company and the company he worked for as a salesman claimed to have never had him in their employee."

"Do you think he just went home to his other woman?" Naomi asked fish-ing for more details about the Nashville harlot.

"He probably had her on the string to. I don't know just when he took up with her."

"So, how did he end up with you here in Kentucky?"

"In an effort to find him and get him served with his divorce papers, I called home from Paducah and asked Aunt Molly to leave him a note on the highway thirteen gas station bulletin board back by the map. He was always fascinated by that four state map every time we went in there, when we were first married. He found the note after we had been separated for two years. He then made his way here to Kentucky to once more interrupt my life and sweet talk me into taking him back never once mentioning he had a pregnant whore in Nashville."

"Had his hair grown back out?" Naomi asked.

"He wasn't back in my life for two months till he again shaved his head and got a tattoo of a nude woman on one arm and a navy anchor on the other. I was totally pissed. The shaved head thing was what we had separated over. Plus, I found the nude woman tattoo to be very offensive."

"My Joel never had tattoos. They would have been considered graven images and sinful." Naomi replied realizing that in getting the tattoos, he had made up his mind to never return to her or their community. She had waited for him for five years for no reason.

"Let me tell you, Naomi . . . the nude tattoo was sitting on his upper arm with her legs spread apart flaunting her flower, to put it nicely. I was totally humiliated and knew that I couldn't parade him bare armed in front of my elementary school students. He overnight, became walking porn and the stranger danger that I was warning my young elementary students about. In spite of the fact that I was crazy about him and had always been in love with him, I realized that he was not going to ever fit into the respectable world and life that I wanted. I secretly excluded him from any school functions happening. I always told my fellow teachers he was out of town, at a sales convention, or something. I was ashamed of his new look. He changed from the once extremely handsome man to a back street, gutter, biker, bar type. I started drinking when I realized how bad I had screwed up my life by taking him back the second time. He had turned into white trash, Naomi."

"I am sorry he turned into such a sinful man." Naomi replied simply. The two years Karen and her Joey had been separated, he had been on the farm with her and she was pregnant with her Mary on the end of it. She also knew that he got the nude tattoo after he walked away in the morning rain heading back to Karen leaving her and her unborn child dying in the floor of her kitchen, after kicking her pregnant belly till she was about unconscious.

"Why did you take him back, Karen?"

"I had every intention of divorcing him. I was saving my money for a down payment on an apartment complex, the one we now live in. The bank kept turning me down for a loan saying I needed a larger down payment. Another individual also had a bid in on the complex and was ready to buy it if my deal fell thru. Joey waltzed back in on the day the bank turned me down carrying a roll of cash. He said it was his checks that he had saved all the years we were married to put down on us a house someday. I was impressed. I thought he had been lying to me about the money. He had somewhere around seven thousand dollars in the roll. I told him if he wanted to stay and try again, he would have to give the cash to me right then to put down on the complex, as well as get a steady job and be at home every night."

"Did he give you the money?" Naomi asked knowing that they had sold their crops and livestock that fall for that amount. She had worked the fields with Joel while pregnant for that money. The Amish didn't have pay checks. They sold their crops and livestock once a year and the large amounts made were their wages to live on for the next year.

"He plopped it down in my hand with big promises to get out and get a steady factory job. I was a fool. The job never happened and he once more got a job as a traveling salesman. Then it was too late. He had his name on my apartment complex deed and I was back to having a traveling salesman wandering in and out. My new life and Paducah dreams went down the toilet."

"How about your two friends you came to Paducah with. Are you still friends with them?" She asked knowing the story of how Karen's Joey had tried to seduce her friend Edna years ago.

"One of my so-called friends married the music major student from here. The other works as a secretary for Dan Maynard, the attorney. My one friend married the music man just to flaunt him in front of me. She was always jealous of me in high school and then college. Her marrying the rich dude was her way of getting at me. That humiliation wasn't enough for her. During the last few days of my marriage to Joey, I walked in on her and my Joey in the basement in a compromising position. She had her hand down the front of his unzipped pants. I threw her out of the basement telling her that I was going straight to her husband and tell him. She left, but Joey was angry with me. He tried to make me the bad guy. Our domestic violence incident made its way to the front lawn of the apartment complex and someone called the cops. He tried to blame his being caught with her on me. He spouted in front of the whole world that I wasn't doing my part to satisfy him in the bedroom. I was pissed and the fight was on. Anyway, I would never let that particular friend be a part of my life again. She purposely played around with two men she knew were important to me."

"I am sorry. Do you care to share with me her name so I can avoid her should I ever run into her?"

"This is the current kicker, Naomi. She has had a secret lover for the last three or four years and it was not my Joey, her husband, or the music major that she was interested in. Do you really want to know who she is and who she has been the married lover to? You might be shocked."

"Yes, tell me. Nothing shocks me anymore."

"Her name is Jenkins and she and Marcus were lovers till you came along."

"Jack has hinted about Jenkins and Marcus being lovers. I am currently cooling my relationship with Marcus for that reason. He rolls in the hay with many married women and I fear that is all he is interested in from me." Naomi replied.

"I have wanted to tell you about Marcus, but I was afraid of losing your friendship. I dumped my friends when they tried to tell me about Joey. I was afraid Karma was going to bite me."

"Well, let us start our walk toward the river." Naomi stated with Karen following her down the flights of stairs from the third floor.

Naomi then forced herself to keep a straight face as they walked and talked. She told herself that she could not show any emotion or cry. Every bit of information she could come up with about Joel, from Karen, could possibly be used by her attorney. She had to keep a clear head and sort whatever facts they were discussing. Karen was a talker or as the English put it, a motor mouth.

"It feels good to let it all hang out. I don't share my nightmare world with Joey with my teacher friends. I don't want them to know anything about him, if I can help it." Karen spit out.

"A little venting and clearing of our thoughts is a good thing." Naomi stated.

"I am once again trying to rebuild my world. Jack is respectable and my first step forward. I am no longer sixteen, young, and pretty. My options for creating a new world aren't what they used to be. My body hasn't been bikini or halter top material for years."

"Jack is indeed respectable." Naomi replied. "The two of you have been lucky to find each other. You would not throw him away for another blind moment of being a fool and taking your Joey back once again?"

"Finding out about his Nashville whore and his secret kids did it for me. I don't believe in love anymore. I now believe in respectability and choosing a mate you are compatible with. I am going to marry Jack, if he asks me. My birthday is coming up. I am hoping for an engagement ring."

"You are still married. What about your divorce? Shouldn't Jack at least wait till you are single to give you one? Are you expecting or putting the cart in front of the horse?"

"We English aren't so uptight about details like you Amish. If he gives me one, I am going to let my divorce go thru. I have been holding it up trying to hold on to my apartment house and not give Joey half. Maybe it is time to let go and move on. Jack owns the building that his apartment is above. I would still have a roof over my head and my job as a teacher. Jack is the respectability that I have always wanted. I will give him all the sex he wants and embrace his world. Every detective needs a sexy wife to come home to and a bed ready for passionate love making. At least I would know he was coming home."

"You English talk so openly about sex and passionate moments. I do not know what passionate love making is. My Joel never made passionate love to me. I was a nightly convenience to him. To be honest, I would like to one day experience what passionate love making is like, if God sees fit to give me a second husband."

"Changing the subject, why has Marcus abandoned the market? Jack tells me he hasn't been there in weeks. Have you called his home to check on him, in spite of Jenkins? He might be ill."

"I do not have a phone, nor do I call men. I am married." Naomi replied simply. "Also, an Amish woman does not chase after a man who has a woman. If I had known last year that he had a three year lover, I would not have set up my display next to him and befriended him. Did you know he once told me that he would never take me home to meet his mother? I am an uneducated farm girl, and not his type. If I was, he would be happy to introduce me to his mother. I was a fool last year befriending him."

"I could have swore that Marcus was nuts about you, Naomi. I also honestly thought that Jenkins had lost him to you, and I was secretly pleased with that. I am sorry things have turned out the way they have between the two of you. Jack told me about Marcus' nephew bad mouthing you and Marcus doing nothing about it."

"At least I am not a fool this summer . . . ." Naomi replied pausing, "And neither are you. We are moving forward with our lives and hopefully you and I both will not take the past back."

"My past is history, Naomi. Both of us are almost thirty and our maturing has let us see clearly what we really want. I want respectability."

"I want to be free from my nightmare past and a mentally crazy husband. I guess I want freedom to love again and have a real life as a woman. I have not slept with a man in almost seven years, plus, my mentally mad Joel is the only man I have ever slept with. I did at first think that one day Marcus and I might become a couple. I was naïve in thinking so and didn't know about Jenkins."

"Dan Maynard's sister, Mavis, told me a couple of weeks ago that Marcus paid his way thru college with money he earned servicing married women. She says that Marcus was a well paid gigolo till Jenkins came along."

"A gigolo . . . I do not understand the term. What is a gigolo?"

"A gigolo is a man who has sex with a woman for money or other expensive items such as clothing cars, or college tuition. Sometimes it is sixty or seventy year old women whose husbands have died or are temporarily between male companions. They are willing to pay well for a young lover."

"Are you telling me that Marcus was a male harlot before Jenkins came along?" Naomi asked big eyed and not wanting to picture Marcus in the beds of elderly women, much less young ones.

"That is what my friend Mavis told me. She found out about his shady side by accident. Do you want to hear the story?"

Naomi bit her lip. "Yes, tell me. I do not wish to be in the dark concerning him."

"Mavis walked in on her seventy-six year old aunt unannounced and found Marcus in the raw in bed with her. Mavis quickly dialed 911 thinking Marcus was some young rapist. The cops came by the time he got his clothes on. Her aunt refused to press charges stating to the police that they were lovers. Mavis immediately checked her aunt's accounts and found that she had written checks over a long period of time to the university paying for most of Marcus' master's degree program as well as the down payment on the jeep he drives."

"He is a harlot like his sister." Naomi retorted in total shock.

"I am afraid so, Naomi. As lonely as I am, I would have paid him on Thursdays for an hour of his time knowing what I do now. He is one gorgeous hunk of a man. He has to be good in bed or the women wouldn't keep calling him back and paying the big bucks to have him."

"Why did he befriend me? I have no money. What did he expect to get from me?" Naomi asked in shock thinking of the moments they had shared fritters and coffee.

"Even a man, who sells himself, occasionally wants a roll in the hay with a woman his age. He probably doesn't get satisfied with the older women. A gigolo satisfies his client, not himself."

"I am glad we have taken this walk and had this talk." Naomi stated as they stopped to peek in a book store window. "I must be a blind cow. I thought Marcus was a respectable man who lived in the suburbs and grew gourds for a hobby. Never would I have suspected that he was a male harlot. I am flabbergasted!"

"I was too when I heard it."

"Why did he give up being a male harlot for Jenkins? Is she somehow more special than me, you, and the rich women who bought him?"

"Considering he had a three or four year secret affair with her, I would say he was in love with her. Prostitutes and gigolos have hearts just like you and me. They fall in love. Having sex with rich women or men is just how they make their living. Jack told me that Marcus asked Jenkins to leave her husband, marry him, and move to California with him a few days before meeting you. She turned him down. He may have originally intended to use you to make her jealous."

"You do not know how that thought saddens me."

"He is probably still in love with her, if the truth were known. My Joey fell for her and her hand down the front of his trousers. I am sure she had her hand down the front of Marcus' too, if you get my drift."

"Thank you for telling me all of this. I know it is gossip, but I am thankful for the information. I might have become a blind cow thinking Marcus was seriously interested in me. After my divorce, I will be very careful concerning who I let my heart race for."

"Smart women are careful, Naomi. They check out the men they date before they sleep or become attached to them. I should have had Joey checked out when I first met him. Molly was dating a cop back at that time. He could have easily ran a check on Joey and saved me ten years of grief."

"You have been a good teacher on this walk. I will not forget. Have you run a check on Jack?" Naomi asked as they walked along the sidewalk in the business district.

"You're darn right, I have. To my surprise, even though he has been Marcus's best friend thru high school and college, he lives a pretty dull, ordinary respectable life. Until the last five years, he was a policeman. His parents died in a car accident when he was in his senior year of high school. He was their only child. He took the insurance money from their wreck and put himself thru college on it and bought the old business building down town that he lives in. His bills are paid on time and he has good credit. He has never been married. Once a year he flies to the islands and comes back home with a new wardrobe of floral island shirts and a new panama hat. He and Marcus were raised on neighboring farms and grew up being best friends. He became a policeman and Marcus became a gigolo. Jack comes from a Baptist background. His mother was a Sunday school teacher and his father a deacon in the church. He has never attended church regularly since leaving home, but isn't anti-religion. He attends church for Easter and Christmas services. He has no tattoos on his body or paintings of nudes hanging in his bachelor pad. My detective told me he is a really nice guy who just had never met the right woman."

"Your detective, in my thinking has painted you a correct picture of Jack. However, he left out the fact that he can't tie a straight tie. His neck tie is always crooked." Naomi replied.

"I will ask the detective for my money back stating that he missed that important information." Karen snickered as they stopped to look in an antique store's window at a couple of antiquated, painted, profile portraits of who knows whom.

"Whoever painted their portraits was smart. He painted only their good sides. I bet the woman has a huge mole on the other side of her face and the man is probably missing a tooth on his other side. He is presenting their best side." Naomi commented looking at the two profile paintings of a middle-aged couple.

Amused, Karen snickered. "I would love to hear your critique of Joey's paintings. Did I ever tell you that he was an artist?"

"No, you have not told me about that. What did he draw?" Naomi asked once again fishing for any tidbits of information.

"When we got back together, after our two year separation, he took up the hobby and set himself up a studio in the basement of the apartment complex. At first, he painted farm scenes with herds of dairy cattle and several canvases of a little Amish girl chasing orange butterflies. Eventually he started to paint portraits of women and nudes that he kept hidden away from me because none were of me."

"Did you know any of the women in the portraits or the nude paintings?" Naomi asked trying to learn all she could about Joel and the ten years which he was married to her and Karen plus had a family in Nashville.

"I recognized one of the nudes when I found the paintings and I blew a fuse."

"Would you like to tell me about that one?" Naomi asked fishing for more information.

"I went down to the basement one morning when he was gone on one of his so called sales trips. The screw on my mailbox had come loose and I needed a screw driver to tighten it. While in the basement poking about searching for a screw driver, I wandered into his studio thinking he might have set our small repair tool box down in there. On the floor of his studio sat a closed cardboard box that had not been there before. I innocently thought he had bought me the new microwave I had been wanting and was hiding it in his studio till my birthday. The cardboard box was the right size. Naturally, my curiosity got the best of me and I peeked." Karen stated pausing to peep at some turquoise hi-heels in a shoe store window.

"What was in the box?"

"I found the box to be full of small canvas paintings of nudes and all of them progressive aging ones of the same woman, his whore in Nashville. The paintings were dated. He had been painting her for four or five years. That was the day I finally wised up to the fact that he had another long term relationship with a woman out there that I had been blind too. I hired a detective to follow him. The detective reported back to me that Joey had children and a common law wife in Nashville. He had two kids that had been born during the five years he was living with me in my apartment complex. He wasn't a salesman. When he left me here in Paducah, he was going home to her and his kids."

"Do you still have the paintings or did he take them when he left?" Naomi asked hoping she would be able to get a peek at them.

"I took every canvas he had ever painted in our basement and slashed them with my kitchen butcher knife and then sent them off with the garbage man. All the nudes he painted were probably of women he had affairs with. I can see it now. I was such a blind idiot, Naomi."

"Does his studio still exist in the basement?"

"I have been meaning to clean out his painting supplies down there and trash them. I haven't done it because I just don't want to have to go down memory lane looking at his stuff and then possibly have to hide in a bottle again. I don't want to reopen that old can of worms. Maybe thirty years from now, I will go down there and throw out his paints or any canvases I might have missed. There are a couple of closets down there in his studio I didn't bother to explore. I was so mad that day that I just took my butcher knife to everything that was readily available and then dove into a bottle of vodka till he returned from his so called sales trip."

"How did the paintings of the Nashville woman end up in your basement? Would it not have made more sense for him to have stored them at her place?"

"My detective says their landlord threw him and his whore and everything they owned onto the street curb for not paying their rent. She took her kids and moved into a women's shelter and he apparently made his way here with what was the most important to him, his paintings of her. He didn't manage to hide them before I saw them."

"Would you like me to help you clean his art studio out?" Naomi asked hoping to get a look at where he painted after leaving her half dead in her kitchen floor and killing their children. She just needed to know the truth about her nightmare so she could find some closure to all of her questions as to why he did what he did.

"Thanks for the offer. However, that studio, and all that is left of him, can sit down there and rot."

"I understand. I had to turn my back on my Amish life and leave it behind to rot not looking back. We do what we must to survive."

"Chocolate . . . I need chocolate. I am trying to quit my Saturday night binge drinking. That is the reason I asked you to take this walk with me. I am having one of those nervous, out of control days and it is not my monthly causing it. I got a letter from Joey today. He wants to come home. This is a bottle of vodka night and Jack isn't here to hold me and keep me from it. Joey now has a third child with the Nashville whore and he wants to come home. What I should do is forget about his paintings and use my butcher knife to cut off his male thing. I read in the newspaper that some chic out in California actually did that last week. She made a girl out of her man while he was sleeping."

Naomi snickered. "Do you still have the newspaper? I think I would like to read about it. Nothing like that ever happens in the Amish community."

"You have got a lot to learn about English men, Naomi." Karen replied in a know it all voice and rolling her eyes.

"And you have a lot to learn about an Amish man, also." Naomi replied.

Down at the river, they sauntered along the water wall and looked at the murals picturing life on the river. Karen continued their conversation.

"Did I ever tell you how I met Joey?"

"No, but I am listening. You have listened to me over the months speak of my mentally ill husband."

"There is this convenience store back home that sits on Highway 13 that Aunt Molly goes to for gas and other small purchases. I was almost seventeen and had just graduated high school. Aunt Molly was pumping gas and I went inside to use the girl's room and then get a cold soda. I had been helping Aunt Molly mow the lawn and had on super skimpy short shorts and a halter top to stay cool and get a tan as I mowed.. There was this young Amish looking guy standing back by the rest rooms studying a map that was on the wall. He looked to be about seventeen or eighteen, my age. He was the best looking hunk of a guy that I had ever laid my eyes on in his funny little no-zipper pants and his funny straw hat. It was love at first sight on my part. I just walked up and asked him if he was lost and if I could help him find what he was looking for on the map. He turned, eyed my short curly red hair, and then looked up and down my suntanned body. I knew I had his full attention. We talked a few minutes and then he walked me out to my Aunts car, after I paid for my soda. He quickly asked me if he could visit me out at my Aunt's farm. I had showed him on the store's map where I lived. He told me that he had just got off at the store and that he had left a northern settlement and was new in the area and looking for work. Every day for about three weeks, he would show up right after lunch and stay till about four. It was a whirl wind romance and we were married on the lawn of Aunt Molly's house after about three weeks. We then lived with her while he wandered about in the city near us looking for work."

"I see." Naomi answered biting her lip. She was pregnant with Adam when Joel married Karen illegally. Apparently, it was Karen he loved; not her or the baby of his that she was carrying back then. She had only been married to him for five or six weeks.

"We then moved into the city where he got a job as a truck driver and I got on at a fast food restaurant. He would be gone a week and then wonder back home for an overnight stay. We were young lovers and lived and breathed to be in each other's arms. For the next three years he wandered in and out of my life claiming to be a truck driver and then a traveling salesman. I am sure now that he was going home possibly to the Nashville whore that he had stashed somewhere in Missouri."

"Let us indeed buy a couple of chocolate bars. I think I need one also.

Your husband's betrayal of you has made me sad." Naomi replied knowing that it was also the story of her betrayal.

Naomi and Karen walked away from the river front and made their way to the business district where black wrought iron benches were scattered along the sidewalks to sit on. They chose one in the shadows near the downtown bistro after purchasing a couple of candy bars from a vending machine. Then they sat down to talk further and kill some Saturday night hours.

CHAPTER FOUR

Marcus' Married Lover

As Karen and Naomi positioned themselves on their bench in the shadows of the bistro to chat awhile, a teal colored jeep passed.

"Wasn't that Marcus' jeep?" Karen asked pointing to a jeep parking down by the river in public parking.

Naomi turned her attention that direction. "Yes, that is him." She said watching him get out and her heart jumping into her throat. She was mad at him, and disgusted with who he was, but he still made her heart race. He was very handsomely dressed in a dinner jacket and tie. She had never seen him dressed up before. She liked the way he looked, but at the same time was mad at her-self for having a racing heart. She now knew he was an adulterous man, a gigolo.

Then Naomi choked on her last bite of chocolate as she watched Marcus help a woman out of the passenger side. Her racing heart plummeted into her clunky, black, old lady shoes. She gasped for air and Karen slapped her back a couple of times. After clearing her air way and regaining her composure with a couple of coughs, she watched Marcus offer his arm to his lady friend. Naomi wanted to die on the inside.

"Are you okay?" Karen asked.

"I . . . I am okay." Naomi whispered trying to regain her composure as they sat in the shadows of the bistro, the town's most expensive fine dining restaurant.

Karen glanced back up and at Marcus in the distance thinking she might yell at him for help if Naomi continued to choke. Then she saw what Naomi's problem was. Marcus in a black dinner jacket and tie had a familiar bleached blonde bimbo, wearing a black cocktail dress and spikes, on his arm. She knew the blonde, but was not sure whether Naomi did.

"Is she your friend?" Naomi asked lowly. "Is she the one who had her hand down the front of your Joey's trousers?"

"Yes, that is Jenkins. I guess their love affair is on again and that is the reason for his not being at the market. Her husband is out of town right now. He is settling some relative's estate back East. Mavis told me about it. Jenkins and Marcus have probably been rolling in the hay, as you put it, every Saturday morning he has been gone."

Sitting on the shadowed bench, trying not to be noticed, they watched Marcus escort the blonde from the river front parking lot up the street to the bistro. She was all over him with roaming hands.

"One more asshole shows his true colors . . . !" Karen spit out. "I could have sworn last fall he had a thing for you. However, it is not you on his arm for dinner this year. "

Naomi suddenly felt really alone and depression hit her like a ton of bricks. She was an ugly farm girl that Joel didn't want and that Marcus had played some sort of sick eat fritters with me game. In the moment, she saw herself as ugly and a woman that no man would ever want. She had no bottle to crawl into and forget. She had to face her ugliness. Her racing heart was dying a very painful death in the moment watching Marcus with his married lover enter the bistro.

"I am a fool, Karen. You were right. Apparently he used me to make her jealous enough to come back to him. I am just an ugly, uneducated farm girl that will never have a man love her. I am looking at a lifetime of being alone after my divorce. I am not sure that I can face that. I wish in this moment that I had died with my children."

"I wish I had died the day before I met Joey." Karen replied. "Forget Marcus. He isn't worth your getting depressed over. He is what he is and you are what you are."

Naomi rose and then threw her candy bar wrapper into a trash bin behind the bench.

"Let us take a peek thru the front glass of the bistro at their dessert display. I feel an urge for half of a chocolate cake coming on, not that my hips need it." Karen stated walking out from the shadows. Naomi followed. "Then we will wander down and check out the window of that new little dress boutique that went in where the shoe repairman was last year."

"Alright . . ." Naomi stated following her to the bistro window.

As they were peeping at the dessert display in the window, the bistro's door opened and Marcus and Jenkins stepped out almost bumping into Karen and Naomi. Marcus looked shocked seeing them. Jenkins in her black cocktail dress and spike shoes immediately grabbed Marcus's arm, marking her territory with her roaming hands.

"Well . . . , don't the two of you look all snuggly and cozy! I gather your husband must be out of town." Karen smirked facing her old friend Jenkins who was holding to the arm of Marcus and then quickly added. "Are the two of you an item again, or are you still seeing my husband?"

Marcus looked at Naomi who was not saying anything. "This is not what you think, Karen. Jenkins needed an escort tonight for a university social gathering. We were just here to drop off an order for a birthday cake for a friend of ours. What do you mean asking Jenkins if she is seeing your husband?"

"Just in case you don't know, while she was seeing you, she was also sleeping with my Joey. You are a fool Marcus. I walked in on her and my husband when you had only been seeing Jenkins for about a year. She dumped you and wouldn't go to California with you because she was seeing someone other than you that apparently was probably a better lover." Karen shot back with her jittery monthly emotions on edge. What she was thinking was coming out of her mouth. "Everyone in town knows you are a damn gigolo, Marcus. I know it and so does Naomi."

"Well, if you can't afford a gigolo, it is not my fault." Jenkins retorted. "You should have married better."

Marcus dropped his head and closed his eyes. Karen had just laid him low in front of Naomi. His past was now all hanging out. How did he now explain Jenkins on his arm for the night? How could he tell Naomi that he did not know she was coming along, or he would not have lived the loose lifestyle he had. How did he explain that he had spent the last few Saturdays turning male tricks to come up with enough money to buy her an engagement ring. Jenkins was paying him for attending the social event and favors afterward.

Trying to save himself, Marcus quickly stated eyeing Naomi. "I am a single man. If I choose to go to dinner or anywhere else with a woman, it is my business. I am not going steady, engaged, or anyway promised to either of you, nor do I feel I owe either of you an explanation for my being with Jenkins."

Naomi took a deep breath. He had no right to put her down. She had been standing there silently listening to Karen vent and get into it with Jenkins.

"You owe me nothing, because you are nothing to me. However, in God's sight you are an adulterer and a male harlot. I am sorry I have wasted my friendship on you. You are a dirty man in the eyes of God who sleeps with old ladies and whoever else will roll in the hay with you. I am not a roller like the adulterous woman you have on your arm, nor will I ever be."

Jenkins let go of Marcus's arm. "Have you been seeing this plain Jane farm girl?"

Marcus didn't answer but stared at Naomi who had just stomped him into the dirt with her words.

"Cat got your tongue?" Karen asked Marcus seeing that Naomi had got to him.

"Stay out of this, Karen. This is between me and Naomi. I am single, Naomi. Who I choose to date is my damn business. Preach to someone else. I am not in the mood to hear the voice and words of my mother. You are just like her and yes Jenkins is right. You are a plain Jane, uneducated, idiot of a farm girl that is pissing me off right now. Who I am or who I have been is none of your damn business. I have never stepped one foot inside of your apartment with you since we have known each other. I have reasons for everything I have done in my life to become the respectable man I am here in Paducah. Now back off and get out of my and Jenkins way." He stated mad.

"Have you told Jenkins that you told me that you are in love with Naomi?" Karen blurted out in defense of Naomi.

Naomi's eyes got even bigger and she bit her lip to control her tongue.

Marcus's mouth dropped open and he was in shock that Karen would have revealed that.

He didn't say a word but just stared at Naomi.

"You are in love with that Plain Jane farm chic?" Jenkins asked letting go of Marcus's arm. "What do you see in her?"

"You do not have to worry about Marcus being in love with me. He is like a worthless wild dog. Any old bitch of a dog, wild or tame, is fine with him. He will roll in weeds or the mud with any ugly,un-pedigreed bitch of a dog who wanders along."

At that point, Jenkins instantly slapped Naomi. "I am not an un-pedigreed bitch." She yelled.

Marcus then quickly stepped between Jenkins and Naomi not wanting Jenkins to further attack Naomi who was a full head shorter than Jenkins.

Karen stepped to Naomi's side.

"Slap me, you bitch. I have wanted to pull every hair in your head out ever since I caught you fondling my husband's man thing in the basement of my home. I dare you to slap me. When you do; I am going to go for your face with my nails and it will take five plastic surgeons to fix your face when I am thru with you."

"Karen, back off!" Marcus half yelled not really knowing what to do. He had three women about to get in an all out cat fight.

"Karen is my friend," Naomi then stated loudly regaining her composure after being slapped. "I now know that you, Marcus, are not. She has stood up for me and you have stood for Jenkins. I never wish to speak to you again. Come Karen. The two adulterers are not worth wasting our time on." Naomi stated and then she and Karen walked away down the sidewalk toward the river.

Marcus yelled after her holding on to Jenkins to keep her from lunging and going after Naomi. "I never want to speak to you ever again either, you Amish bitch. I hate your clunky, black shoes, gray dress, and your constant preaching to me like my mother. I don't need a second holiness mother."

When Naomi and Karen were a good half block away from the bistro; Jack step out of the shadows of the bistro with his camera in hand to confront his lifelong friend Marcus.

"Well pal," he began. "I once told you that if anyone ever disrespected Naomi I would be knocking their teeth down their throat. In this camera are photos of you and Jenkins and her pawing every inch of you tonight. When I leave you, I am taking the photos straight to her husband who hired me to follow her. She won't be married to wealthy, Mr. Music Man afterward. That is the best punch in the teeth I can give her."

"Please, Jack, don't do that!" Marcus begged. "I will lose my job at the university. He has clout."

"I just heard you call Naomi degrading names and telling her you hated the way she looks. Also, I heard you yelling at her that you never wanted to speak to her again. She is my girl now, and no one disrespects my girl." He stated pulling his arm back and sucker punching Marcus sending him sprawling backwards onto the pavement. "I told you I would knock anyone's teeth out that ever disrespected her." He then sprinted away to catch up with Karen and Naomi.

"Get up and defend me, you ass hole." Jenkins stated pulling on Marcus' arm. He was on the ground rubbing his jaw and seeing stars. "You let that damn detective leave here with those photos. At least chase after him and get the camera."

"It is all over, Jenkins. My world and yours has just tumbled down around us. Jack was just telling me like it is. I deserved the punch."

Down the block, Jack caught up with the two women in his life.

"Wait up." He yelled as he got close enough for them to hear him.

"Where did you come from?" Naomi asked as her and Karen turned to greet him.

"I was following Jenkins." He stated resting a minute, being out of breath from the sprint.

"You should not be running. Remember, you just had surgery last spring."

"It is my knuckles that are hurting, not my incision." He stated laughing.

Karen threw her arms around Jack's neck. "You hit him, didn't you? You took our part."

"That I did. I just decked my best friend and now have the pleasure of walking by the river with the two prettiest girls in Paducah." Jack stated rubbing his knuckles.

Naomi bit her lip. She was almost at the point of tears concerning the whole event. She did not believe in violence, but was pleased that Jack had stood by her. Marcus had chosen to stay with Jenkins and stand by her.

"You should not have hit him Jack. I deserved the slap I got. I gave in to my emotions and called his date a dog."

"I heard. You can't be faulted for telling the truth. She is one. Right now, she has three men on the string plus her husband who will soon be her ex. He hired me to follow her. In case you are wondering and so it won't be a surprise to you, your Joey is one of the three. She is driving down to Nashville and meeting him in a motel every other week."

Karen's face lit up. Her music major man had wised up. At the same time, she instantly became sad. Her Joey had a common-law wife in Nashville with kids and was also secretly seeing Jenkins, the woman she had thrown him out over.

"Thanks for the information Jack. I will tell my attorney. Jenkins was the final straw that broke me and Joey up. I walked in on them together in my apartment house basement?"

"Her husband has discovered that and wants a divorce without having to pay her alimony. Three men on the side and years of giving Marcus big sums of money should do it." Jack smirked.

"Would you and Naomi mind walking by the river by yourselves? You can drop by later when you are thru. I want to call Aunt Molly before she retires and update her on this choice bit of gossip. When we were in college back in Missouri, my aunt tried to tell me that Jenkins was making eyes at my Joey. I didn't believe her at the time. I owe Aunt Molly a long overdue apology."

"Do you want me to drive you home?" Jack asked. "My car is in the riverside parking area."

"No, I will walk. I want to think about what I am going to say to her. Our relationship has been strained for the last ten years because of Joey." Karen stated. She then kissed Jack on the cheek and left him and Naomi standing a block down from the bistro. "I will see you later."

After Karen had left them, Jack offered Naomi his arm. "Come on Sweet Thing! I need a quiet walk by the river to make my knuckles feel better."

"I need a pleasant walk by the river to calm my Amish temper. I was wrong in calling her names, Jack."

"In my book, you will always be right." He smirked. "My Sweet Thing has a little bit of sass in her."

"I will read my bible for two extra hours as a punishment for my slapping mouth." She stated.

As they headed for the river, they did not see Marcus following in the shadows behind them. He had told Jenkins to catch a cab after having words with her.

"Have I told you about a crazy dream I had a few days ago?" Jack asked.

"Do you wish to share it with me?" She asked.

"I dreamed I was at the farmer's market and there were two crazy angels there chasing a skunk. One angel was black skinned and the other was white. The bigger of the two angels was waving a huge nail file at the smaller one and yelling something about loving a long legged Jack Rabbit. In the crazy dream, I kept you safe and you asked me to hold your hand. Now, I just kept you safe from the blonde bimbo and Marcus and you are on my arm."

"In shock, Naomi asked in a low voice, "Was holding hands all we did in the dream? I am a married woman and you do have a girlfriend."

He looked her way, patted her arm that was linked in his with his free hand, and grinned from ear to ear. "Don't ask about that part of the dream. You just might make me do a month of Bible reading."

Naomi bit her lip and then took her free hand and placed it on top of the one he was patting her arm with and gave him a little embarrassed smile. She could not tell him that they had shared the same dream. "Whatever you have dreamed about me; has to be a good thing. I am okay with you dreaming good things about me. However, the question is; will Karen be okay with it?"

"I am going to continue seeing Karen till after your divorce. When the polygamy case crap hits the fan and she finds out she has no legal claim to Joey and his assets and that I am the detective that has brought her world down, she will see me as a traitor and dump my ass. In the meantime, with her on my arm, I can come and go freely helping you in your apartment with your baking and other chores. You don't need to worry about there being anything between Karen and me. We are in a going nowhere relationship. Someday, Naomi, your heart will quit racing for Marcus. Till then, I am a patient man."

"I don't know what I would do without you, Jack. You are the only one who truly knows me and has stood by me. Marcus stood by Jenkins tonight. Deep down, I wanted him to take my part in my little, sinful cat fight with Jenkins. He did not. I have been a fool thinking that he and I might be a couple someday. It is you that has continuously stood by me. I will try to silence my heart concerning Marcus. I know that it is you that I should love."

"I am willing to wait for your heart to race for me. In the meantime, you have got to put up with me and the redhead."

"You do know that Karen is hoping for an engagement ring for her birthday."

"She will just have to be disappointed. The only woman who will ever wear an engagement piece of jewelry from me wears little white ribbons hanging from her bonnet." Jack replied as he pointed to a bench in the shadows of the river wall for them to sit on.

Naomi looked at him and blushed as they seated themselves. "What if my heart does not quit racing for Marcus?"

"I will live with it, but I will also always be in the background of your life, should you ever need me."

In the shadows, Marcus lurked watching Jack and Naomi. He was totally outraged when his best friend Jack put his arm around Naomi's shoulders and pulled her up close to him on the bench as they watched the river flowing beyond them. Never once had he got to walk down by the river with her or felt the touch of her arm linked in his, much less put his arm around her shoulders. Now his best friend had her on a bench, in the moonlight, and was making a move on her and there wasn't a damn thing he could do about it.

His little dinner at the bistro rendezvous with Jenkins had cost him big time. In his mind, he wanted to sprint out of the shadows, confront Jack, and snatch Naomi out of his arms. Instead, he knew he had to go home to Angela's three kids that he had been stuck with for the last three or four weeks. Angela was in a rehab center drying out. She was lucky she had not gone down the river to the state penitentiary for giving drugs to her newborn. Marcus had temporary custody till she got out of the drying out facility for drunks. Plus, he had to think of some way of explaining away his past as a gigolo to Naomi. At the same time, he wondered who had dared to gossip and tell her. He had been pretty good about keeping his night vocation a secret over the years. He watched as Jack leaned the side of his head against Naomi's. He had never been jealous before. Women had always flocked to him; that is everyone but Naomi. He had never had to compete with anyone for a woman. However, he saw that his best friend Jack was one up on him. His friend had Naomi in his embrace. Marcus' eyes filled with tears knowing that she was the one, the only woman he would ever love and he was a piece of gigolo crap who was a month behind on his jeep payment because his sister had finally depleted his savings with her last drunken fiasco. He knew that he was going to have to work the night shift to overcome his bad financial situation. Also, if he was going to stand a chance against Jack, he had to have money to buy Naomi an engagement ring and plop it on her finger the day her divorce came thru. He was not going to let his best friend steal her from him.

Reluctantly, Marcus left the shadows down by the river and drove away having three kids to pick up from a baby sitter.

In the invisible, Osceola and Frankie Frances stood guard behind the bench where Jack and Naomi sat in the moonlight watching the flow of the river and listening to the night sounds.

"You are not doing your duty, Ms. Osceola Black Lightning. You let that blonde tailed dog reach out and slap Naomi with its paw." Frankie Frances stated sharply in her sticky, syrupy, honey dipped, bee swatting voice. She then pushed her glasses back up her nose. Her glasses never stayed in position. Her nose was like a greased sliding board.

"I am doing my duty, Frankie Frances. When I want your opinion, I will ask for it. At the moment, I don't recall asking." Osceola retorted in her syrupy, sticky, fly swatting voice.

"You never ask; that is why I am forced to offer it to you. I am a resource that you are not using." Frankie Frances returned in her honey dipped, stinging bee voice. "You are an angel that God did not know what to do with. I have heard gossip amongst the other angels about how crass, uneducated, overbearing, and big mouthed you are. None of the other angels has an assistant. That means you are not capable of performing your duties like the others. It is time you started to listen to me. You are like a human special needs child on Earth. You need a little assistance and a patient teacher. God was very gracious giving me to you. I am his favorite angel, in case you haven't figured it out. He wouldn't give me to just anyone."

"You little witch . . ." Osceola retorted in a mad fly swatting voice. "You know as well as I do that you were thrown out of Heaven for putting your dog walking leashes on a band of demons, mistaking them for dogs, and then walking them away from the throne of judgment and letting them escape. God stuck me with you, not blessed me with you. The special needs child is you. I am a death angel who opens and closes the gates to hell and you are lucky I don't take you straight there and get rid of you. I would enjoy slamming a gate of Hell in your face."

"Testy, this morning, aren't you." Frankie Frances replied. "I know better, Ms. Osceola Black Lightning. I was the best Hounds of Heaven walker that ever did doggie-doo duty in God's Garden. This Earth assignment to help you is a promotion. In my opinion you have been demoted. You just don't want to admit that you are a failure and need me to straighten you up and get you going again."

"You are in for a rude awakening, motor mouth. You are in for a serious dose of reality, and the White Suit is going to be the deliverer of it; when his angel shortage isn't occupying his mind. I think he plans to demote you to being Heaven's shoe shine boy."

"I don't see that as a demotion. Think of all the cute male angels I will be helping. It is every girl's dream to have a barrack full of good looking men at her beck and call. I will be older when that promotion comes thru. Just think of all of those gorgeous male hunks fighting over who was taking me out on Saturday nights. I will have an extremely handsome hunk on my arm just like Jack has the most beautiful lady in Paducah in his embrace tonight."

Osceola rolled her eyes as they continued to stand guard behind Jack and Naomi. She was going to give the White Suit a piece of her mind when she got back home for sticking her with the motor mouth that was full of her-self.

"You didn't answer my earlier question. Why did you let the blonde dog slap Naomi? You are supposed to be guarding her. I would have swished and swayed my sword and broken every finger on her slapping paw. You are not doing your duty, in my book." Frankie Frances stated in her young, honey dipped, bee stinging voice.

"Naomi deserved the slap. Just because you are Amish, it doesn't give you the right to judge others or call them names. She used sly words to call Marcus and Jenkins dogs. Naomi deserved what she got." Osceola stated in her syrupy, sticky, voice.

"That was an error, Ms. Osceola Black Lightning. God will get you for it. Jenkins guardian angel will probably be in trouble also for letting her be a slapping pawed dog."

"Jenkins doesn't need a guardian angel. She has ruled and guarded her world for years. Only wimps need guardian angels. Someday, Naomi will find her inner strength and she won't need us. She will guard her world. I actually admire Jenkins for setting Naomi straight." Osceola replied to the shocked face of Frankie Frances.

"I am making a list of your duty infractions, Ms. Osceola Black Lightning. I am sure that God will be real happy to see how close of an eye I have kept on you. My list will probably get you demoted even further. You should watch your step with me. I am going to hold you accountable for your every miss-deed."

"Throw your list away, Frankie Frances. God does not need lists. He sees everything including your mouth and unbelievable ego this evening. I would watch myself; if I were you. He just might assign you to an all female barracks of angels and there wouldn't be a male face within three planets of you. He has put all of the northern United States between me and my Jack Rabbit."

"He is punishing you, Ms. Osceola Black Lightning. What were you doing with that long legged Jack Rabbit man when God eyed you? Were you committing fornication? That is a biggie sin with him."

"That is for me to know and you not to, Frankie Frances. Matters of the heart and body are private."

"I have a plan to get around God's spying eye, when I return to heaven. God is busy on Sunday mornings listening to all the Earth's church folk pray and beseech him. I plan to date my angel men during that time when his eyes and ears are full of people needing Him. If you need some hints as how to not get caught committing fornication, I will be most happy to share them with you. When was the last time you had a little loving? It has to of been a long time, because you are one sour, foul mouthed, moody, unsociable angel most of the time."

"You are thirteen going on fourteen. Discussing fornication with you is not appropriate, nor is the discussing of my love life. When you are fifty and I allow you to date, then you can discuss the subject with me. Till then zip your mouth you filthy minded, little female angel pervert." Osceola retorted in a harsh voice. She was sure that she was going to stuff one of Marcus' gourds in Frankie Frances' mouth and then strangle her to death before her mission of guarding the white caps was over. Frankie Frances was really getting on her nerves.

"You are a know- it-all, Ms. Osceola Black Lightning; one who has seen her best day and is soon to be sent to live in a nursing home hell for crazy, old angel has-beens. They will lock you in and throw away the key."

"I carry the key to Hell, Frankie Frances; in case you have forgotten. Picking a nursing home hell lock would be child's play to me. Besides, the day I go into a nursing home is the day you start shining shoes in God's all female military barracks. You better pray my assignment down here lasts a longtime. Shining shoes will age you fast." Osceola retorted in her syrupy, sticky, fly swatting voice.

"Now don't go and get all bent out of shape. I am just trying to be nice and help you. You are just jealous of me and I know why."

"You think I am jealous of you? What could I possibly see about you that I would be jealous of?" Osceola replied annoyed.

"Earlier, I opened my eyes wide and took a real good look at the back of Marcus in his tight fitting, designer dress pants when we were down by the bistro standing in the shadows. You squinted to take a look at him. I saw you. You are jealous of my eyes." Frankie Frances stated pushing her slid glasses once more up her nose and into position."You need glasses. I got the better eye full of his backside and you are jealous about it. You are jealous God gave me special glasses to see with."

"You thought his blonde headed date was a yellow tailed dog. I dare say you were looking at a pair of parking meters and thought they were his legs and backside." Osceola retorted fully aggravated with her young assistant's over-inflated image of herself.

"My glasses had slipped when I was eyeing Marcus' date. You can't hold that against me." Frankie Frances stated as she glared at Osceola.

"Well, did you have your glasses and eyes in adjustment when Marcus and his date came out carrying two white objects from the bistro just before the cat fight?"

"Yes, my glasses were in position and I saw the two beautiful white Persian cats they were carrying. Why?" Frankie Frances shot back.

"Your two white Persians were two white, foam containers of to go food." Osceola retorted in a pleased, sticky voice knowing she had just stuck a deflating pin into the ego of Frankie Frances.

"You don't like me and are always picking on me. You are an over the hill, has been, death angel who wouldn't know what to do with her long legged Jack Rabbit even if she could see his back side in jeans." Frankie Frances replied in a huff looking for anything to dig Osceola with.

"You are an under the hill want-to-be who can't see two feet in front of her nose. You will marry an ugly man someday because you are too blind to tell a Persian cat from a box of fried cat fish." Osceola stated, not surrendering in their war of words.

"You are mean!" Frankie Frances stated and then stuck her tongue out at Osceola.

Osceola rolled her eyes. Then she pulled her nail file from her pocket and gave it a minor swish and sway. Instantly, Frankie Frances had a dog muzzle on, preventing her from speaking or sticking her tongue out. Frankie Frances went to wailing, crying, and trying to take the muzzle off.

"A little lesson in silence never hurt anyone." Osceola muttered. "However, I should have stuck a pacifier in her mouth before I put the muzzle on. Now she sounds like the cross between a squawking parrot and a mad howling wolf."

CHAPTER FIVE

Song and Dance

A couple Friday nights after the Saturday night cat fight incident, Marcus was free again. Angela had come on the bus to get her kids. She couldn't get food stamps, housing, or a welfare check without them after being dismissed from the rehab house for alcoholics. Once more, Marcus had a little money in his possession. He had done the double duty to get it. However, he had found that servicing the married women had not been as easy as it had been before Naomi. With each woman he slept with for money, he heard Naomi's voice preaching fornication and adultery to him. He had so hoped to hide his past from her. Having to reopen his can of worms, his life as a gigolo, was an unexpected one. He had to have money to feed Angela's kids as well as bail her out of jail and pay for attorney fees again. It had been a long five weeks not seeing Naomi. Also, much to his dismay, he was on a round of antibiotics. One of his married women had given him a case of the unexpected. He wasn't sure which one had passed the disease along to him. Even worse, Jenkins had it and was on antibiotics. He had given it to her, in his thinking. His returning to the night world of the gigolo had not been a pleasant one. However, he did have enough money stuck back to buy Naomi a fairly nice engagement ring, if he shopped the pawn shops. There was no way he could afford one from a jeweler. He had barely got his back payment on his jeep caught up.

Weeks had passed since Adam had mouthed Naomi and the cat fight with Jenkins had occurred. Adam and Jenkins had spoiled his new farmer's market season with Naomi, sucked him dry of finances, and had prevented him from participating in the market which was his love. He had not been able to afford much in the way of baby sitters, so he had to stay home on Saturdays with Adam, Mary, and Martha. He had to have his baby sitting money to cover his being away from home at night when he needed to go out to make money. Now the kids were gone home, Angela was clean, and hopefully he could get his life afloat again. He knew that Jack had did everything possible to take Naomi away from him while he was indisposed. He wasn't sure how far his friend had gotten. He tried not to think about it. Somehow, he would make Naomi love him in spite of Jack. The weeks away from Naomi had been torture. Every woman he slept with, he pretended she was Naomi. The life of a gigolo has lost its appeal to him.

After pulling on a new pair of jeans and a sports logo T-shirt from his closet, he pulled out a new pair of sneakers from a box, laced them up and then put them on. Mary had taken an ink pen, when he wasn't looking, and drew on the toes of his old ones. It felt good to get dressed and be his old self again without Adam and Mary living and breathing to see what they could get into. He hated to admit it, but he was glad the three had gone home. They had none of the values he hoped to instill in his own children. They were foul mouthed, rude, hadn't been trained to go to bed on time or eat at a table. His weeks of sudden fatherhood hadn't been pleasant.

It was Friday night and He knew Naomi would be baking for the Saturday market. He decided he was going to climb the stairs to her third floor apartment and beg if he had to, in order to get back in her good graces. He also regretted yelling that he hated her black clunky shoes and that he didn't want another version of his holiness mother. He had dug himself a hole that he was sure was not going to be an easy one to get out of. He was going to have to lie and insist that whoever had told her that he was a gigolo, had him mixed up with someone that looked like him. He decided to ignore the subject of Adam. That incident was too far in the past to add to the current equation. Hopefully, she had accepted the fact that he was single and did have the right to date till she committed to him. That would halfway get him off the hook for having been out with Jenkins. Jenkins being married was not something he could explain away. It was what it was. This time he would bite his lip and hold his tongue, no matter how much she preached to him about adultery and fornication.

Marcus stopped on the way to her apartment and bought a sheath of summer flowers for Naomi. His heart was racing and at the same time, he had the nervous jitters. He had never had to explain himself to a woman or beg. This was a first. Over and over in his head as he drove, he practiced what he was going to say when she opened the door before she had a chance to slam it in his face. He peeked in his rear view mirror and checked out his new hair cut. He had made an effort to look his best, but casual. He wanted her to walk down by the river with him, the reason for his casual dress. Jack was going to have to move over. He was reclaiming his girl.

Parking his jeep in front of her apartment complex, he picked up the sheath of flowers from his passenger seat, got out of his jeep, and headed up the stairs to the third floor apartment. Reaching the top, he took a deep breath and then knocked. He could smell her breads baking. He wanted that smell coming from his kitchen and kids of his own to go with it. The smell coming from her apartment was what a home should smell like.

Marcus knocked a second time and suddenly the door opened and to his surprise, Jack stood eyeing him and the flowers.

"Are those for me?" Jack smirked.

"What are you doing here?" Marcus asked in shock. "Where is Naomi?"

"She is busy mixing a bowl of raisin bread dough. I am here helping her wrap bread and put on stickers, if it is any of your business." Jack replied watching with delight his friend squirm. "I am here because I have a date."

"Not with Naomi, you S.O.B. I haven't forgotten your punch or words. I have had my sister's kids for five weeks and unable to see Naomi, you back stabber!" Marcus stated mad and throwing the sheath of flowers down. He hadn't expected to find Jack on the other side of the door. Naomi didn't let men in her apartment.

Suddenly, Naomi wearing a full white apron stepped in front of Jack. "I am whose woman?" She inquired not smiling.

"Er . . . uh . . . , I have come to apologize."

"Your apology is late, weeks in coming and I do not wish to hear it. Take your flowers and give them to Jenkins. I have no need of anything from you." She stated wiping her floured hands on her apron.

"Damn it, Naomi, what is it about this sucker that you let him in your apartment, but not me? Remember your Amish tenet about not being alone with a male other than your husband. Well, what will your absent husband think about him?" Marcus sputtered with his pot of emotions boiling over.

"You date and sleep with multiple married women. That is compounded fornication and adultery. You shame me coming here. I am not one of your roll over in the hay women, nor do I want you on my door step taking a new peep at my ugly shoes."

"I am sorry I said that, as well as comparing you to my mother. I was mad. You called me a dog and preached to me. I am here to say I am sorry. You and your Amish faith do believe in forgiveness don't you?"

"You let your blonde lover slap me and stayed comforting her when I walked away from the Bistro. You did not abandon her and walk away with me or fetch ice from somewhere for my face. You yelled at me and insulted my shoes. My shoes are mad and they do not have to forgive you. I must walk in them, so I am on their side."

Marcus suddenly saw the humor in what she said and bit his lip to keep from laughing. She was wonderful in spite of the fact she was angry with him.

"So, I must make up with your shoes?"

"Yes, you owe them an apology. Furthermore, you let your foul mouthed nephew say awful things to me weeks ago. You did not discipline him for it, nor made him apologize. I have been weeks without your friendship, caring, or apologies. Perhaps I was wrong in calling you a dog. However, for the first time in my life, I stood up, opened my mouth, and said what I thought. I had no Amish or English man to tell me I couldn't. As you put it, you were single and had the right to date her. I was single and had the right to speak my opinions. Now, I am telling you that it will be a cold day in Hell before I ever give you, your nephew Adam, or Jenkins the chance to walk on me again. I think that is how the English say goodbye forever."

Karen stepped up to the door hearing the altercation of words. She had been busy washing some baking pans.

"Well, look what the cat has dragged in!" Karen smirked. "Where is your dinner jacket? Are you slumming tonight? I gather you think my plain Jane friend Naomi, with the ugly shoes, isn't worth the dinner jacket treatment?"

"If it will make you happy, I will go home and put it on! I am single and I had a reason for taking Jenkins to dinner." He sputtered wishing Karen would back off and shut up. She wasn't helping matters.

"My husband fed me lines of bull to cover his sneaking off to be with other women. Excuses don't fly around here. I was with Naomi and saw the married blonde bimbo hanging all over you and running her hands all over you. Naomi and I were sitting in the shadows on a bench and watched the two of you walk from the river parking up the block to the bistro. At one point, I believe she had her hand on the front of your fine dining trousers. You are a piece of gigolo crap, Marcus. Mavis told me all about your little escapade in her aunt's bedroom."

Marcus turned red and turned to Naomi. "Naomi, please. I have come to apologize!" He begged, trying to ignore Karen who was not backing off. At that point, Naomi started to close the door in his face. He quickly stuck his foot in the door blocking it. "I am sorry Adam bad mouthed you. I am sorry Jenkins slapped you. I didn't intend for you to get slapped. I didn't intend for Adam to bad mouth you. I am sorry, really sorry!"

"Goodbye Marcus. I have learned where your allegiance lies and Jenkins is your choice for a friend, not me. I have not seen you for weeks. She has." Naomi stated once more starting to close the door. "I do not play second hand fiddle. Please remove your foot from my door."

Marcus didn't move his foot. "Just lay it on the line and tell me what you want in order for us to make up. Do you want me to kiss your feet, crawl, beg, or sleep outside your door for a week? Just tell me!"

"You did not take me to dinner or provide me ice for my face when I was slapped. Jack was there for me, not you. I should never have befriended you in the first place. You are not Amish, nor are you a respectable man. Goodbye, Marcus."

"Please Naomi, if we can't go back, can we start over again? I have missed you."

"No, we cannot. I might have got over our words concerning Adam, but I cannot look past Karen's friend telling us of your being in bed with a woman three times your age. The thought disgusts me. Watching your married lover run her hands all over you, as you walked to the bistro down town, was equally as disgusting in my eyes. She has a decent husband. However, I do apologize to you for calling you a dog. On the other hand, I am disgusted with who you really are. You are a male harlot, a shame in God's eyes. He does not condone such behavior, nor do I. You are what you are and I am what I am. What I am not is one of your married women who will roll over in the hay with you or pay for your services. I am sorry I found out how sinfully dark your life is. The Marcus who ate fritters with me and tasted my jelly was a good man. Now, I see that the fritter and jelly taster was only a mask you wore. I do not embrace or condone sin and darkness."

Jack stepped in front of Naomi." It is time for you to take your foot out of the door." Jack sated eyeing his friend. "If you try to force yourself in on her, you will have to go thru me."

Pissed, Marcus turned and left yelling at Jack. "You are a back stabbing traitor. You know how much I love her."

CHAPTER SIX

The Cold War

The summer, farmer's market season was in full swing. It was late July and there was a cold war going on between Naomi and Marcus, who had once been friends. They both stayed on their separate sides of the market aisle, not speaking. Marcus ducked his head, every time Jack or Naomi caught him looking their way. Naomi, on the other hand, totally ignored Marcus; never glancing his way.

Naomi had a year to put in of silence and staying clear from men. Jack, as a friend, was okay because he was dating Karen and never came to her apartment without her. Since the evening on the bench by the river, Jack had made no further comments about his having feelings for her. Naomi figured that his continuous dating of Karen had bonded them and they were becoming more than Jack had planned. She was okay with that because secretly, her heart had never stopped racing for Marcus, although she intended to have nothing to do with him.

Naomi knew she could not do anything that might affect her divorce proceedings. Her children deserved justice and headstones on their graves. Although she had feelings for Marcus, she was glad they were not speaking. She was not free to tell Marcus why she was pushing him away, because of his sister. Also, being aware he dated married women for money, she feared his feelings for her were not honorable.

After her divorce, Naomi knew that she would have to start over again somewhere, due to all her friends' having connections to Joel. Jack would probably be her only remaining friend in Paducah when the dust settled. Dan Maynard's words continued to play in her head telling her that her friends were the ones who were standing with her in the end. Although she was enjoying her girl hours spent with Karen, she knew that Karen and Marcus would be those who turned on her. She was trying to think ahead and decide where she should start over in another city and state, or whether she should just stay in Paducah and ignore anyone walking away from her. She did have her business started and it was doing well. However, she knew how to do it all over again. She had honed her selling skills, as well as improved her products.

July ended and then August. Then the last week of summer rolled around. Naomi rose early to make sure she got to the market on time. The Saturday market was her only social outing where she was free to converse with male customers as well as female. During the week, she cleaned her rich ladies houses, baked on Thursday and Friday evenings with Jack, and enjoyed Karen occasionally helping her. The rest of the week, other than going to the market, she stayed in isolation. Now, her year of waiting was creeping to a close. It was September and she only had to make it to spring, and it would all be over.

Mr. Maynard informed her, on a visit to his office in August, that Joel was in St. Louis bouncing back and forth between two unsuspecting wives there. Also, he presented her with photos of other illegal wives in Illinois, Indiana, and Ohio. He reminded Naomi to continue her code of silence and avoiding being seen with any man alone. He also told her that it was possible Joel had a couple more women on the string that he was dating and planning to marry above St. Louis in Iowa. She was shocked, but she no longer cried. He also told her that her polygamy case was one of the biggest things to ever come across his desk. Naomi only saw it as a nightmare.

It was still dark outside when Naomi eased her rolling tote down the three flights of stairs to head for the market. As she reached the bottom, she stopped for a moment to straighten her load and make sure her breads were not being crushed. The profit, from each loaf of bread sold, fed her for one day. Her money from cleaning houses paid her rent and attorney fees. Every carefully packed item in her tote was important. She desperately needed new shoes and had been saving her change for a pair. She had duck tape covering cracks on the bottom of the pair she was wearing. However, she had priorities. The saving of money to get a divorce had been more important than shoes. However, she knew that her shoes would not make it thru another winter. She had worn them every day for three years. They had been mended, patched, and duck taped, till there was nothing to mend and patch. She had a can of flat black spray paint that she used on them to cover scuffs, duck tape, and patches to keep them presentable. She was looking forward to having a new pair of shoes to journey forward and past her divorce in. She had paid her dues for a new life somewhere. Wearing worn out shoes and the same two dresses for three years had been part of those dues. Her under-things and black socks were equally as bad.

As she was checking the load in her tote, a voice spoke from the shadows.

"Good morning. I have brought coffee."

Naomi spun around to see where the voice of Marcus was coming from.

"What are you doing here?" She asked in shock. They had not spoken to each other for months.

"Don't say a word, Naomi. I don't want to hear it. I am here to walk you to the market and pull your tote." He said forcing a cup of coffee into her hand. "I cannot bear your shutting me out of your life. I want you to forgive me and wrinkle your damn nose at me, so I can fall in love with you all over again. I want you to be my friend again. You may be able to live without me in your life, but I cannot do so without you. Don't say a word. I don't want to hear about how I have let you down and how much you hate me. I just want to share a pleasant walk with you to the market and say the things to you that I should have said long ago. I love you and I am sorry for everything that transpired last spring and early summer. You were right about Adam, Jenkins slap, my loose morals, everything. There I have said it. Please love me again!"

Marcus reached down and grabbed the handle of her rolling tote. "We are starting over!"

"And just what do I get for the wrinkle in my nose that once was slapped out of shape?"

"Naomi, don't go there! I can't go back and change that moment. All I can say is that I am sorry and mean it."

"Jack is my friend now and I wrinkle my nose at him only." She retorted as he pulled her cart along.

"What do you want? Just name it and I will do it." He replied pulling the cart with one hand and sipping his morning coffee with the other. "I have no intention of letting Jack or any male take you from me. You may not love me, but I am madly in love with you. I am trying everything in my power, including begging, to get you to forgive me and fall in love with me. Please. Naomi, give me a chance? Just tell me what you want me to do to make things right with you."

"I do not wish to interact with your nephew on Saturday mornings, nor do I wish to interact with your married lovers. Your words, telling me you love me, mean little to me because I wonder who else you are saying them to. If you want to start over, you will move your gourd display across the center aisle of the farmer's market next to me. It would be a sign to our vendor friends that I have won the cold war with you. They are all aware that your nephew mouthed me last spring and that you let Jenkins slap me. I will never set up next to you again or have you cart my table." She replied taking a sip of her coffee which she had missed. "However, I cannot help who sits up next to me at the market. Don't expect a lot from me, because I do not see you the same as I once did."

He stopped with the rolling tote and moved to stand in front of her looking into her eyes. "I know I let you down last spring. I am fully aware of that. Your shunning me has been a life altering experience. I never wanted you to know about my married lover, Jenkins. If I had known you would pop into my life one Saturday morning at the farmer's market, I would have waited for you and never dated her. I am sorry."

"You are what you are and I am what I am, Marcus. I do not condone adultery or fornication, nor do I feel the need to interact with disrespectful children. These are my boundaries. If you want to renew our friendship, then you must not expect me to embrace that which I do not feel is right in the sight of God."

"If I move across the aisle and admit to all of our market friends that I was the cause of you dumping our vendor booth friendship, can I join Jack and Karen on Friday evenings helping you bake? I have apologized to jack."

"No. It means I will share fritters and coffee again with you on Saturday mornings and we will start over. I am married and my husband is away. Your telling me that you are in love with me is not appropriate. Coming to pull my tote is also not appropriate. However, I am in need with the tote this morning and welcome my special coffee. I have missed it. If you want my friendship, Marcus, you must abide by my Amish rules. My husband has reentered the picture and I am not at liberty to have a man declare he is in love with me. I am married. You must not use those words in my presence."

"Naomi, I know about you sleeping in your closet with a butcher knife and a flashlight. Karen told me the night I leveled your stove. I know about your husband walking out on you and how your two children died."

"I do not wish to discuss my marriage, my husband, or my children under any circumstances. I am here to start over. Why I sleep in a closet is my business. The English world is new and scary to me. I feel safe in the closet. I do not have a husband, father, or brother to protect me here. I must protect myself. The closet is a safe haven."

"Please let me be a part of your life, Naomi. I am willing to be anything. You may not believe my words, but I don't want to live without you. I know you are that special one that comes along only once in a lifetime. I love you."

"Well, you loved your special someone named Jenkins, more. I seem to recall you letting her slap me and then standing between us so that I could not slap her back. I am now making it just fine in the English world on my own. I have made it without a bother, husband or father. I do not need you to be anything to me. I thought I needed you when I first met you at the market. I now test my own jelly and corn relish. What feelings I had for you died when you let your married lover get by with slapping me and your nephew disrespect me. I have no need to love you again as a friend. However, I am willing to make you a fritter and share a cup of coffee with you on Saturday mornings."

"Your terms are acceptable as long as you give me another chance. I want a life someday with you, Naomi. You can dictate the terms of how we get there."

"My husband did not want me, nor ever wanted me. I have saved my market money and now have enough to divorce him in the spring. Till then, I am married and live by the tenets of my faith. Unlike you, I do not sleep in someone's bed that I am not married to. I am not a fornicator or an adulterer. Those standing with me after the day of my divorce, I will consider to be my friends. If you are standing with me at that point, then I will consider a deeper friendship with you. The proof is in the pudding." Naomi stated sipping her coffee.

"My mother uses that same phrase. I used to try to impress her by telling her of my hopes and dreams as a kid. She would reply the proof is in the pudding."

"I am sorry I have never met your mother. I am sure that we would like each other."

"Just so you know, I broke my relationship off with Jenkins just before I met you. She dumped me, if you want to know the truth. You came a long a few days later and I was so thankful she had. I have been in love with you since the first time you smiled and wrinkled your nose at me. I am laying my cards on the table with you, so there aren't any secrets between us. Also, I did sleep with Jenkins the evening you saw me at the bistro with her. I had my reasons for doing so and you have got to realize that there has been no commitment between us other than friendship. I am also sorry you found out about my sleeping with older women. When I was going to college, I needed money to pay for my tuition and books. I did not have a free ride thru college like Jack had. I didn't want to owe my parents anything and therefore be obligated to embrace their lifestyle. I did not know that one day you would come along and I would have to explain my reasons for doing anything. You are the first woman ever that has made me shuffle my feet like a thirteen year old explaining why I have stayed out past adult curfew. I think it is only fair that you forgive me for Jenkins and the others. They were before today. When Jenkins and I made our way to the bistro, I had no idea I would bump into you there or that you knew about her and the others."

"I found a special friend in that moment, that I did not know I had. Jack has taken your place with me. He was there for me, after I was slapped, and held me in his arms down by the river, when I needed to cry. He loves Karen, but he has proven his friendship to me. He will be the only man that steps foot in my apartment till my divorce. It will be him and Karen that helps me with my baking or whatever else needs to be done."

Marcus bit his lip. The thoughts of Jack, being in her apartment all summer, had driven him crazy.

"What part of you can I have? As bad as I hate to admit it, I am willing to play second fiddle to Jack. I will take you in whatever form you are willing to give me. Please, Naomi . . . give me another chance."

"I am getting a divorce and do not wish to be seen in any compromising situation with any single man. All I am willing to give you is an apple fritter on Saturday morning. If you move across the aisle to where I am, I cannot help who sits up next to me. The market is a public place. I am on the countdown to spring and my court date. My husband has been found. Furthermore, you are a man who has lived a life of fornication and adultery, your nephew is a little imp in human flesh, and you did not stand up for me in my words with Jenkins. I have no intention of falling at your feet and kissing your shoes or even considering you for anything beyond friendship. You may be a prize to all of your married lovers, but you are not to me. You are an adulterous man who has tried to keep his sins hidden till now. In this moment, if you and Jack were the only two men left in the world and I had to choose between the two of you, I would choose respectability and that would be Jack."

"You are definitely a carbon copy of my mother, Naomi. However, I will admit that you and my mother are the type that I would want raising my children someday. I just didn't know it, till I met you last fall. You are going to make a damn, holiness, front church pew sitter out of me like my father, aren't you? That will be your price for loving me!"

"The word damn does not fall from the mouths of front pew sitters. You are a back row man right now. Jack is a front row man."

"Jack uses the word too when he is teed off."

"He does not use it in my presence. He respects me. You do not. In my opinion, I feel you see me as an uneducated farm girl that you want to use for a cheap roll in the hay to make your Jenkins jealous so she will take you back. I don't play roll over games. I am the one thing that your married adulterous lovers are not. I fear my God and I believe there is one man for one woman for a lifetime unless there is adultery involved. That is Bible principles. My husband has been found in another state living with another woman and has children by her. I have a right to a divorce. I will be single in the spring but will still live by the tenets of my faith. Should I meet a man and wish to marry again, I still will not sleep with him before my wedding night. How many adulterous wedding nights have you had? Marriage is not a piece of paper. It is the coming together of two people in the sight of God. I will not lay on my back with many and have my God eyeing me while I do so. You should be ashamed of your past and all the women you have defiled for money. One of them will not be me."

"Just lay it all out there. I am hearing you, mom." He replied half angry, but trying to control it. His mother preached to him every time she called. He had moved far away from home to get away from his religious nut of a mother and her narrow views. Now, Naomi had taken her place and he was squirming like a guilty thirteen year old in her presence. He had been running from his roots and family values. With Naomi, he could not run anymore. She was what they were and he was in love with her.

"Someday, I would like to meet your mother. She must be a wonderful person. If I am like her, and she in embracing moral values; that is a complement you have paid me. One should always honor their father and their mother."

"It is you that I love enough to change for." He said as he pulled her rolling tote into the flea market and then helped her set up her table and display.

Jack had been absent from the market off and on all summer. He told Naomi that he was working on one of the biggest cases he had ever been on and that he was following leads in four states. Before leaving last Monday, he had given her the key to his apartment and told her to go there if she had to exit her apartment suddenly. He was her confident and knew how serious the repercussions from her divorce could be. He had been the one who helped her make up her mind to approach Dan Maynard about starting divorce proceedings. She appreciated Jack. He never failed to stand by her.

Even though she had deep down feelings for Marcus, she knew a rekindled friendship between them would not last. His sister and Karen were the reasons her two children were dead. Karen she could forgive, but Karen would not forgive her once her apartment complex was in jeopardy. Marcus' sister was a whore with mouthy children that she did not intend to socialize with. She knew that Marcus would choose them when the chips were down. They were his blood kin. She also knew that she would choose justice for her two dead children over him. She just needed to get thru the fall at the market and then make it to January or February when her year was up.

After helping Naomi set up her display, Marcus walked across the aisle and then moved his gourds and seeds across the center aisle and set up his display next to her. Naomi knew that he had really sacrificed his pride in abandoning his vendor booth spot that he had used for years. However, she could not let him get to close or alone with her because of her year of silence and Mr. Maynard's instructions for her not to be alone with any man. That part she could not tell Marcus. She had to keep him at arm's length till her year was up. If he stood by her, when his sister was subpoenaed, she would let him get nearer to her heart. However, she was one hundred percent sure that he would abandon her when her marriage to Angela's common law husband was exposed.

After their displays were set up, Naomi watched Marcus as he walked to a round metal trash can that had a metal lid. He removed the lid and held it like it was a shield. Returning to his booth, he retrieved two unused milk crates and placed them one on top the other in front of her booth. She was not sure what he was up to. Then he picked a long necked gourd from his display and climbed on top of the milk crates standing tall. Holding the trash can lid like it was a shield, he began to beat on it with the long necked gourd making a terrible pounding, dull metal sound. All the vendors stepped out of their booths into the center aisle to see what he was up to.

"Hear ye . . . Hear ye, all those dwelling in the land called the Farmer's Market." Marcus shouted when he stopped beating the gourd on the lid. "I Marcus Plum went to war with one Naomi Toombs. Being defeated in war, I hid in my cave fortress, where my booth used to be, trying to ignore her and win a cold war. She has prevailed and won the war between us. I now fly my white flag of surrender. Hip – hip – hip hooray for the great, conquering warrior, Naomi Toombs. She has won the farmers' market war and I am now her spoils. She owns me, my shield, my gourd sword, and my white flag. I now kiss her feet and openly declare that I am her slave and that she can do with me as she pleases! "He yelled. Then he started to beat the metal trash can lid again with his gourd as everyone cheered, clapped, and laughed. When the laughter and clapping died down, he quit beating the trash can lid, took a bow, and then jumped down from the milk crates. He then put the lid back on the trash can where it belonged and removed the two milk crates from in front of Naomi's booth.

Naomi was all smiles. He was fun and she was not used to being with a man who made her laugh. He pleased her very much with his little display, although she wished he had not done it. She had months to go before she could be seen with a man or have one declare his intentions. She hoped no one having anything to do with her case had witnessed the event.

After waiting on a customer who stepped up to his booth, Marcus stepped behind Naomi's booth and took her hand, raised it and kissed it. "Will that do? Our friends now know that I belong to you and that I have apologized for being a jerk."

"You have pleased me. However, do not kiss my hand in public. Remember, I am married till my divorce comes thru."

"When your divorce comes thru, I am kissing the wrinkle on your nose, your ears, and wherever else I choose! If you don't want me committing fornication with you, then you had better marry me the day after your divorce is final."

"Hush . . . , Marcus! Everyone will hear."

"Shall I get up on the milk crates and declare my intentions to marry you in the spring?"

"You wouldn't?"

"Tell me you love me just a little bit, and I will contain my gourd beating self. Otherwise, it is on the milk crates again for me."

"I cannot tell you I love you because it is inappropriate. I am married. However, if it gives you any pleasure, I like the way you look from the back in your tight fitting jeans. Your long legs in your jeans and your backside please me. Read into those words whatever you like. Will that do?"

Marcus began to laugh. "Thank you! He said taking her suddenly in his arms and hugging her while resting his chin in the top of her white cap. God alone knows how much I love you, Naomi."

She quickly pushed him away. "Marcus, do not hug me like that! Be happy with my words, but keep your distance. We think differently. You, or any man I choose to be with, must not touch me till I am divorced."

"I plan on doing a lot of touching when you come out of the divorce court!" He stated grinning.

"You are awful. Do not even think about hugging or kissing me till you have courted me a year and then knelt on one knee. I am Amish and that is just the way it is."

"At least I know you are in love with my backside. Every time you turn your face toward me now, I am going to flaunt it at you."

"I should never have told you that. You are not going to let me have a minute of peace now, concerning the subject."

Marcus returned to his booth, turned on a portable radio, and started dancing around in his booth making sure his backside was to her.

Naomi grinned and threw a tea towel at him that she used to cover breads with. She could tell that he was pleased. He grabbed it, kissed it, and threw it back. Their friendship was on again.

In the invisible, standing behind Naomi's booth, Frankie Frances turned to Osceola.

"What does she see in his backside? He is just a set of tall, fence post legs covered in denim." Frankie Frances asked eyeing the backside of Marcus with her glasses slid to the end of her nose.

"Well, push your glasses up where they belong and you will see what she sees in him." Osceola retorted and then snickered as she took a good second look at the backside of Marcus herself. "He has long legs just like my long legged Jack Rabbit. If I wasn't already in love, I could go for him myself."

"He is just two fence posts wearing a hoodie!" Frankie Frances replied with her glasses sitting lopsided on the end of her nose.

Osceola reached over with one extended finger and slid Frankie Frances' glasses up her nose into place. "Does he look like two fence posts wearing a hooded sweatshirt now?"

"Oh . . . I see what you mean!" The teen angel replied slowly in her honey dipped, young voice. She then replied with a sigh, "He is cotton candy, peppermint sticks, and Belgium chocolates all nicely displayed in one gold foiled candy box. He is yummy."

"That he is, but he is not the yummy for your tummy. He is taken." Osceola stated in her syrupy, sticky, fly swatting voice seeing that her assistant was drooling.

"I just might ask God for him. I am sure that I am more of a woman than the white cap God has hooked him up with. Sometimes God does make mistakes!" Frankie Frances stated while she held her slippery glasses in place eyeing Marcus. "I can see myself spending eternity with him, shining his shoes, and putting my touch on whatever else he wants shined."

"Frankie Frances, get your eyes back in your head and your drooling dog tongue back in your mouth. God doesn't make mistakes and you definitely won't be shining his shoes or anything else that belongs to him." Osceola replied in her sticky voice as she rolled her eyes. "You are lusting and you are not old enough to do that. Turn your head. I will do the drooling for both of us."

CHAPTER SEVEN

Abraham's Visitor

Abraham Toombs, Naomi's father-inn-law, stood at the rear door of his son Joel's abandoned farm house. He had come to check the doors and have some quiet time away from his farm and wife to think. A detective, he had hired to look for his son Joel, had approached him with news of his son as he was harvesting pumpkins. What the detective had told him was not good news. He dreaded returning to his house and having to tell Martha. The scandal that he and Martha thought had been laid to rest was popping up its ugly head. Once upon a time, twenty-eight years before, his wife Martha had an affair with a neighbor English farmer. To get even, he had pursued and had an affair with the man's wife named Molly. Two babies were born nine months later within a couple days of each other. Martha gave birth to Joel and Molly gave birth to a girl who grew up to have wild red hair just like him. He had kept the red haired baby a secret because he did not want shunned from his Amish community. Joel, Martha's son belonging to the neighbor, was raised Amish. Now, something disastrous had happened and he was going to have to tell his wife about the red haired girl she knew nothing about and the secret life of his son. If word got out in the community of what their son had been up to, they would never be able to hold their head up again. His wife was going to have to admit that everything she had said about and done to Naomi had been wrong. That would be a hard pill for her to swallow.

Molly's red haired daughter, that she told everyone was a niece she was raising, was possibly Joel's half sister. The detective had discovered that Joel had a second wife that he had married within weeks of his marriage to Naomi who lived just a few miles behind the Amish settlement. Their adulterous son had reopened his and Martha's can of worms, unknowingly. His wanderings away claiming mental illness and amnesia had been a deception to cover up his going home to his other wife. His son had managed to live two lives with two women for five years, before abandoning Naomi. Joel's second wife, Karen, was possibly his half sister. He had somehow met and married his father's daughter by Molly. That was incest. With his adultery added to it, his youngest son would be shunned. He dreaded dragging up the old scandal and having to tell his wife of Joel's adultery as well as the fact he had a red haired daughter that she knew nothing about.

His marriage to his wife Martha was in name only. They had not slept together or been civil to each other for twenty-eight years. They pretended to be Amish happy when their son James or members of their community were in their presence. Otherwise, they barely spoke and slept in separate bedrooms. Although they stayed together, they were husband and wife according to the tenets of their Amish faith, but nothing more. They smiled and supported each other when in public, but beyond that they barely spoke.

His lover Molly had tried to keep her pregnancy hidden from him telling him she was getting fat. However, he knew but could not claim his daughter short of being shunned. Now his secret was about to bring him and Martha to their knees and cause them and their son Joel to be outcasts. He didn't know what to do.

Sitting down at Naomi and Joel's handmade slab board kitchen table, he thought about the day an angry English farmer's wife walked in on his Martha and her husband in bed. She had pulled a gun on naked Martha and marched her across three miles or so of farm fields in a blazing sun with a gun held on her. His fair skinned Martha was severely sunburned from the ordeal. Some of the brethren in the fields had seen the spectacle. The scandal had been hard to live down in the community and some of the older women still gossiped about it. Two older women members of the community had witnessed her being marched across their fields as well as some of the men. He had thought the whispering and years of snickers would never end.

Martha had almost been shunned over the event. He went to the brethren and told them that he did not want a divorce; not even on the grounds of adultery admitting to them that he himself had an affair with the woman with the gun afterward to get even with Martha. They both barely escaped their Amish community's worst form of punishment, shunning. He still was not allowed to speak at services or seek to be an elder. He had paid dearly for twenty-eight years; that included not having a woman in your arms at night. He and Martha slept in separate bedrooms afterwards.

Joel, his son, had been a terror to rear. He killed small animals such as kittens and birds without a hint of remorse. He also would take money from his mother's jar where she saved the money from selling eggs. He would walk to town and spend it on candy and soda, with no regard for the fact his mother was saving for new shoes for herself or a coat for him. They had hoped, when he married and had children, he would change. Even though he was the handsomest teen boy in the whole Amish community, with his raven hair and blue eyes, none of the brethren would let their daughters be courted by him. He had a reputation for being cruel to animals and a petty thief. As a child he couldn't be shunned because he had not reached the age of eighteen and joined the church yet. At seventeen, Martha hatched a plan to find him an orphan girl, from one of the northern settlements, to marry. Naomi arrived by bus and married Joel the day after, at the insistence of his wife who was desperate to hide Joel's history from the girl. They were married by a Baptist minister at his wife's insistence. Afterward, Martha told the community Joel and Naomi eloped. Naomi never knew the difference. She was young, naïve, and two days shy of her sixteenth birthday.

Now, Naomi was going on twenty-eight. She was twenty one when Joel walked away into the rain abandoning her. After five years of waiting for him to return, at the age of twenty-six, Naomi walked away after leaving a note asking James to watch over his brother's farm, still thinking that Joel would possibly return one day. She had been an innocent pawn used by his wife to hide their son's darkness. Now, his son had been found by a detective and he had never been mentally mad as they thought. He had taken a second wife just weeks after marrying Naomi, and it was his daughter by Molly. The detective had sucked the life out of him when he was told about Joel's second wife and who it was. Now, he had to decide whether to tell Martha about the detective's findings, or to just stay quiet and hope that Joel never returned.

Until the detective spoke with him earlier, he had thought his son Joel was crazy and had wandered from their farm being schizophrenic. The detective had shown him photos of his son with Molly's daughter plus a common law wife and kids in Nashville, Kentucky. He was not sure what to think about the whole situation. The detective also told him that his son planned to marry the common-law wife and he was not divorced from either of his first two. The detective wanted him to travel to Nashville to attend and stop the wedding to keep his son from being branded a polygamist with no hope of ever returning to his Amish community. He dreaded telling Martha and reopening their can of adulterous worms.

It had been twenty eight years since their affairs. It didn't matter how they tried to overcome the scandal, it just kept popping back up. Now his son had multiple secret wives and one of them possibly being his half sister. If that were to be found out, Joel's coming home to the community was over. What was worse, their son James, who was thirty, would find himself shouldering the disdain of the community and he was not guilty of anything. He was their first child who was conceived on their wedding night. He did not deserve to be looked down on by the community. Abraham Toombs did not know what to do. His whole world looked like it was going to belly up, including Martha leaving him when she found out about Karen. He didn't want to die old alone.

A knock sounded at the back door to the kitchen. Abraham rose to see who it was. Someone had probably seen him enter, possibly his son James. He made his way to the door and opened it and was surprised to see his niece Sarah standing there.

"Good morning, Miss Sarah. May I ask what you are doing knocking on Joel and Naomi's back door?"

"I was hoping that Joel had returned home." She replied smiling. "I stop and knock occasionally, just to see."

Sarah and Joel had bonded as cousins. He was a lot older than her, but had seen her as his pet. She was a lover of butterflies and he was fascinated with her ability to call them and see them land where she said. She had been three or four when he was a teen.

"It has been about six years, Sarah, since he left. I do not think he is going to return to us. He may be dead somewhere."

"That is an awful thought, Uncle Abraham. Have you heard I am being courted?"

"I know for a fact that your parents have been adamant about your friend John not being allowed to court you. Now that you are older, have you fallen in love with someone new?" Abraham replied stepping out onto the back porch to talk to her.

"I am afraid I have not been very respectful of my parent's wishes. I have driven them crazy insisting John is the only one for me and that I will not be courted by, nor marry anyone else. I have gotten up every morning since I graduated eighth grade and at the breakfast table have asked them for permission to be courted by John. I have worn them down and finally my father has agreed. My mother is very unhappy about it, but father threw up his hands and said enough is enough and that he would go to John's father and make the arrangements for our courting. We started our year of courtship a few weeks ago."

"Well, my butterfly loving niece, I hope you have made the right choice. Marriage is forever and I am sure that your parents have had their reasons for not wanting you to court or marry John."

"That is just it, Uncle Abraham, they refuse to tell me their reasons for not wanting us to court and marry. John's parents aren't telling either. His mother does not want him marrying me. Our parents dislike each other for some reason and neither one of us can figure out why."

"Don't ask me if I know why, because I don't. Over the next year, Sarah, just keep an open mind and make sure that John is the one for you. After you marry him, you cannot walk away. Amish marriage is forever."

"I understand. Will Naomi be returning?" Sarah asked.

"No, Sarah, I don't think she will be."

"I wish I could invite her to my wedding; but I can't due to her being shunned by the community. Forgive me for saying so, Uncle Abraham, but I don't believe Aunt Martha's insinuations that Naomi is a witch. Every time I visited Joel and her when I was little, she was always reading her Bible and praying. A witch does not do that. My beloved cousin, Joel, on the other hand, had a handful of photos of a naked, red haired girl hidden in a hole in that big oak back by the blacktop. He spent his free time looking at them instead of reading his Bible and praying. I was out chasing butterflies in the fields and walked upon him looking at them. I asked him about the photos of the naked lady with red hair. He swore me to secrecy and told me that she was the orange butterfly that he chased. I was young and thought if I chased butterflies, it was okay for him to do so. I was only five or six and everything was a game to me. I am grown now and know that Joel was willfully lusting for a woman other than Naomi. When I walked upon him that day, he was staring at his naked girl's photo like she was an idol. He quickly placed them in a plastic container

84

and then put them in a hole of the tree that was way above my reach and swore me to secrecy."

"That is something that you should really not speak of, Sarah. That could get your cousin shunned. He is not here to defend himself."

"I know. That is why I have kept it my secret all of these years. He is not crazy, Uncle Abraham. He has just flown away to be with his butterfly woman. By pretending to be crazy, he can return here when he wants. I know him better than anyone. He confided in me, even though I was really young. He said we were alike and that one day I would fly away too."

"Do you remember which tree he hid the photos in?"

"The tree was huge and stood in the thicket of woods near the black top road on your side of the fence. I remember the tree had the name Karen carved on it. I remember fingering the letters and asking Joel what they spelled. He told me they spelled Karen." Sarah replied.

"Thank you for the information, Sarah. The name may help us find Joel."

"I have got to go, Uncle Abraham. If Joel or Naomi should return, please tell them about my wedding next year and how happy I am."

"I will, Sarah." He replied.

When Sarah was out of sight, Abraham Toombs stepped off his son and Naomi's back porch and started walking toward the back of the twenty acres which had once been his before he gave it to them as a wedding present. It was rough walking. The back of the property had grown up in brush with Joel having been gone for over six years. Abraham did not see someone following him in the shadows.

Reaching the back of the property on the farm's side of the fence, he started walking the fence row looking for a huge tree with a hole in it possibly five to seven feet off the ground, high enough that a five or six year old could not reach. He also looked for a carving of the name Karen. As he moved thru the brush looking at trees, he heard a rustling sound behind him. He attributed the noise to possibly a deer or his farm dog following him. He had walked about five hundred feet of fence line when he spotted a huge tree that was just inside the fence with the black top running the other side. He made his way to it thru the brush, ignoring the breaking of twigs and the crunching of leaves behind him.

Reaching the tree, he walked around it looking for some carving. He spotted a small bare spot on the side of the tree and sure enough, just has Sarah had said, the name Karen was carved there, although it was starting to be overgrown by an Ivy vine running up the tree. He carefully avoided the ivy. He was very fair skinned and just the thought of poison ivy broke him out. Looking upward he started looking for the hole and spotted it about seven feet off the ground. The tree had probably grown since Joel left the last time and the hole had moved higher with the growing of the tree. He looked for something to stand on. He wasn't about to stick his hand in the hole without looking first. A snake, squirrel, spider, or wasp nest could be in the hole. As he was looking about the tree for something to stand on, he noticed that at the base of the tree there was a hallowed out spot in the base and there was something black and plastic looking sticking out of it.

"I know that I am going to regret this . . ." He muttered as he reached thru the poison Ivy vine to get a hold of the edge of the black object. He then quickly pulled and a black trash bag came out of the hole and it was secured at the top having been tied with the lace from a work boot.

He stood for a moment eyeing the bag. It looked fairly old and there were some small holes in it where he had snagged it pulling it out. Taking his pocket knife from his pocket, he cut the bag open to see what was in it. To his shock, he saw a set of Amish clothing. There were pants, shirt, suspenders, farm boots, and an Amish straw hat in it. He held the trousers up and looked at them. They had to be his son Joel's. They looked to be the size that Joel would have worn on the day he disappeared. He picked up one of the boots and looked at it. There was no doubt, his son had changed clothes and hidden his Amish ones the day he had tried to kill Naomi. Abraham realized that there had to be a second set of clothes hidden there for Joel to change into. His son had planned to leave and was not mentally crazy.

Dropping the boot, he returned to looking for something to stand on. There was a fairly good size fallen limb on the ground. He picked it up and then wedged the fork of it against the tree. He then gently climbed up on the wedged limb and peered into the hole that Sarah had told him about. It took a moment for his eyes to adjust. Sure enough, a small weather beaten, sandwich size, plastic container was in the hole. After looking carefully for spiders or other harmful insects in the hole, he reached in and quickly retrieved the dusty plastic container and then jumped down off of the rotten limb that was about to give way with his weight. Once on the ground, he blew dust off of the container and then turned it over a couple of times making sure there wasn't some small spider on it.

Seeing there was nothing on the container that could harm him, he forced the aged, stiff lid off of the container. Sure enough, there were photos in it, just as Sarah had said. He was about to look at them when he heard a voice behind him.

"Is that where you have hidden your pictures of your English whore all of these years?"

Abraham spun around to face his wife. She had her hands on her hips and was visibly angry.

"These are not my photos, Martha. They belong to our son Joel. Sarah came by earlier and told me a story about Joel hiding things in this tree. I have made my way here hoping to find a clue as to why he walked away and hasn't returned. Sarah said he started hiding things here just after he married Naomi."

"Don't lie to me Abraham Toombs. I have seen how you have eyed the English woman when we have bumped into her over the years. I have even seen you wink at her when you thought I wasn't looking. You have never loved me and I have gone thru hell because of you and Joel."

"That is not true, Martha. I courted you for a year, fell in love with you, and married you. I don't know what went wrong between us. After James was born we just got busy with the farm and the routine of married life and drifted away from each other. I am sorry for that, but I did love you when I married you. It was your adultery that destroyed our love and marriage. Leave Molly out of this. She was innocent. She caught you in bed with her husband."

"It was okay for you to have a six month affair with her afterwards? Take a look at yourself in the mirror Abraham Toombs. I am sure you enjoyed using your yanker every night of those six months. This might surprise you, but I never had a chance for the English man to make love to me. We had just stripped off naked and gotten in bed when your whore walked in on us. The son you have denied all of these years is actually yours. The English man never touched me with his yanker. His wife walked thru the door just before we were about to do it."

Abraham turned red thinking about it. He had always thought that Joel was not his. "There is no need for us to dig up the past, Martha. It has been twenty-eight years since we ruined our marriage. We only have ourselves to blame. We did not stick to the tenets of our upbringing. We sinned. You would have enjoyed his yanker had you had the chance. You were in bed with him. We are both at fault."

"Just so you know, Abraham, I hate the ground you walk on. My life with you has been one long nightmare. I have stayed with you because I am Amish. Now, I find you hiding things in trees. Do you have a new lover?" She asked reaching quickly and jerking the plastic sandwich box from his hand. In doing so, the box tipped and about five old weathered snap shots fell to the ground. Immediately, Martha reached down and grabbed one and took a look at it thinking it was going to be of some woman her husband was playing around with. Instead, she recognized her son Joel who was wearing an Englishman's wedding suit and on his arm was a red haired girl dressed in a wedding dress.

Abraham picked a snap shot up from the ground and gasped. It was of a naked red haired girl in a bedroom setting and she looked identical to what Molly had looked like twenty eight years before. He also recognized the bedroom. He and Molly had spent six months in that room making love. He knew every inch of it. The room was etched in his memory. He turned the photo over. It was dated about the time that Naomi had announced that she was two months pregnant with Adam. Naomi had conceived on her wedding night. Suddenly, staring at the naked girl, who looked to be about seventeen or eighteen, he gasped realizing that she had to be Molly's daughter. The naked girl had to be his daughter. She had red hair just like him. He was staring at his own daughter's nakedness. He quickly turned the photo down, quit looking, and closed his eyes in disgust. The detective's findings were correct. Joel had married a second time, when he had only been married to Naomi for a couple of months. Unknowingly, he had married his own half sister.

"God said a man's sins would be passed down from generation to generation." Abraham muttered.

"Give me that . . ." Martha stated jerking the photo from his hand and then looked at the naked photo of a girl that looked just like the woman that had walked her home with a gun pointed at her. "Oh my God. It is her. You have been hiding naked pictures here of your Molly harlot."

"It is not Molly, Martha; nor is it I that has hidden these items. Look in the bag that was hidden at the base of the tree. Tell me if you recognize them."

Martha turned to the dirty, black, trash bag and started to finger the times that Abraham had pulled from the bag. "These are Joel's. I made him this shirt a couple of months before he disappeared the last time. What are his clothes doing here?"

"Our son was not crazy the day he walked away in the rain, Martha. He planned to abandon Naomi, his children, and us. He undressed here and apparently had a change of clothes hidden in the bag here. He changed and hid his Amish clothes in this bag in the hollowed out place beneath the Ivy at the bottom of the tree. The Poison Ivy vine has kept them hidden all of these years. The plastic box of photos has probably been here since Sarah was little. Joel was probably in such a hurry to change and leave that day, that he forgot the box of photos. I rang the bell on Naomi's porch that morning for help after we found her almost dead. Joel may have feared the brethren were being rung for to follow him. He was not crazy, Martha. He planned his abandonment of us."

"Joel would not do that. Naomi cursed him. She was a witch!" Martha screamed holding Joel's dirty shirt to her.

"No, Naomi was a victim of our adulterous son who had another woman hidden out somewhere. The witch's cauldron of milk weed poisoning, that you claimed was on her stove, was just a half made pan of gravy. She didn't get it made. Joel kicked her almost to death."

"You would take up for her!" Martha shot back. "I know about all of the baking days you made special trips to her kitchen to taste her bread. It was not her bread you wanted to taste. I have seen the look in your eyes every time you have looked at her since she arrived on the bus when she was two days away from being sixteen. You shame me, Abraham."

"Me . . . shame you? Don't go there Martha. I do not wish to get in a fight over the woman with a gun who walked you home naked. You had just crawled out of another man's bed. It was you who shamed me. I didn't handle it well and had an affair with her to get even with you. We have been over this a thousand times. I didn't love her. I was getting even with you. God as my witness, I have repented of that deed over and over after every fight we have had since."

"What about Naomi?" Martha asked in a huff.

"What about Naomi? She was our daughter-in-law. We had grandchildren by her."

"I followed you a lot of bread baking mornings and watched you eye her thru her kitchen window. Adam was your child, wasn't he? You are the one who has always had problems with your breathing at times. He had to of taken his asthmatic condition after you."

"Is that what you have thought all of these years, that Adam is mine?" Abraham asked in shock.

"Yes . . . and when I got her shunned, I thought she was out of your life. No . . . you had to secretly sneak around taking her food and knocking on her door on a regular basis. The witch just became more important to you. I knew that was a pan of gravy ingredients. I saw an opportunity to get rid of her and took it. Joel knew she was playing around with you, I told him."

"Oh God, Martha, what have you done?"

"I got rid of a woman who wanted you and my son. I also got rid of your little bastard son, Adam."

"Oh God, Martha, are you telling me you purposely let Adam get sick and die when Naomi was in the hospital?"

"God killed the unrighteous, witches, adulterers, and the first born of the Egyptians in the Old Testament by slaying them. I was just doing God a favor by helping him out."

It was at that point that Abraham Toombs realized that his wife was crazy as well as a secret murderer.

"Did you tell Joel to kick Naomi till she was almost dead?"

No . . . I kicked her big belly till I thought she was dead. I was hiding and peeking on her back porch when Joel pushed her down and gave her a couple of kicks. When he ran across the field not looking back, I entered the kitchen. She had sent Adam for you and then passed out. I kicked her big belly repeatedly trying to get rid of another bastard child that probably belonged to you. I knew you would one day leave me for her. Everyone came running and I just pretended that I got there first. Adam found you out in the barn. I am sure when you ran to help poor, beautiful Naomi that you didn't even stop at the house to get me. You were more interested in getting to her." Martha sputtered mad.

"I am Amish and committed to my vows, Martha. I will be married to you till the day that one of the two of us crosses over. Even if I fell in love with someone other than you, I would not leave you. I did not leave you for Molly."

"No, but you wanted to. I could see it in your eyes. When she walked into a store in the city where we shopped, your eyes lit up. I was aware of your secret winking at her. One affair was not good enough for you. You wanted Naomi too."

"Naomi is my son's wife. I would not cross that boundary." Abraham sputtered mad at the accusation.

"You cannot lie to me. Adam and her bastard baby were yours. I had the right to a divorce or to get rid of her. By all rights, she should be laying in a grave next to Adam and your bastard daughter."

"You are wrong about the children, Martha. They are Joel's. You have killed your own grandchildren." Abraham stated in a shocked voice with a sudden tear rolling down his cheek. "You killed those who would love us and bring joy to us in our elder years. Unless James marries, we will have no one to cling to when we are old."

"I will cling to myself. I don't need you, Naomi, or her little imps. I stopped loving you the day I stood in front of you half naked and you believed the Molly woman's story. You never gave me a chance to tell mine. You just took off across the field with her to peer at what you thought was a lover's bed with my hair pins in it. If you had taken the time to listen to me I would have told you that I was walking along the back road trying to exercise and lose some baby weight. I had not been able to get it off after the birth of James who was one. The gun woman's husband came along in his pickup, stopped, grabbed me, forced me into his pickup, and then into his bed at his farm. He kidnapped and was about to rape me when the Molly woman walked in with her gun. I thought she was crazy and with him. I tried to escape by the bedroom window. I did not take time to get dressed. It was either crawl out the window half naked and run or get raped by the man or shot by her. I was traumatized by the time she walked me across the fields at gunpoint poking me with her weapon. You listened to her and not me. You are the adulterer, Abraham Toombs. It is I who should sue you for divorce on the grounds of adultery. I did not commit it. You did however, for six months. I have lived in a never ending nightmare with you ever since."

"You are making up stories to make yourself look good, Martha." He shot back.

"No, I am telling you the truth, just like I am telling you the truth that I got rid of your little bastards by Naomi. I had the right. An eye for an eye and a tooth for a tooth is what the good book says."

"Oh God . . . what have you done?" He stated once more. At the same time, he wondered if his wife was possibly telling him the truth about fleeing from the bedroom of the Englishman. If she was telling the truth, he was indeed the adulterer and not her. She had stuck it out with him thru it all.

"Take these clothes and photos to the house, Martha. Joel is not dead. I need time to think about what you have said and done. You are old, Martha. You are too old to spend the last of your years in prison for assault or murder. You must not speak of this to anyone. Telling lies on Naomi about her being a witch is bad enough; adding assault and murder to that is unthinkable. Not only could you go to prison, but the community would not forgive us this time. They will shun you and me. Think of James. He is innocent in all of this."

Martha said no more. Abraham gathered up Joel's things, including the photos, and placed them in Martha's arms.

"Go home, Martha. Joel is not coming back. He has chosen a life in the land of the English. If you are telling me the truth about Molly's husband, I am indeed an adulterer and not worthy of you. However, Naomi is innocent in all of this and her children are not mine. They are Joel's. I will swear that on God's Holy Bible just as I am admitting to you that I did indeed sleep with Molly for six months and she has a red haired daughter named Karen that is mine. Naomi's children are not mine."

"What do you mean saying you have a red haired daughter by Molly?"

"I walked across the field mad thinking you were an adulterer and Molly and I consoled each other. Her husband was long gone when we got there. She conceived that night and gave birth to a girl nine months later just as you gave birth to Joel whom I thought was a bastard child. I have a daughter and her name is Karen. She has been a twenty eight or so years' secret."

"I hate you Abraham Toombs. You and your Molly have ruined my life. Both of my sons are yours and I have never cheated on you. I was almost raped, but I have never cheated on you. You have spent a lifetime pointing your finger at me and degrading me. Now, I find out you have a bastard child!" She stated and went to laughing like a woman who had suddenly gone mad."

After Martha took the arm load of Joel's possessions and headed home, Abraham returned to Joel and Naomi's farm house and let himself in. He needed a quiet place to pray and think while he decided what path to pursue to set things right.

As Abraham stepped into the kitchen, he was surprised to find his son James sitting at the kitchen table.

"What are you doing here?" Abraham asked.

"You might say I am visiting what remains of Naomi." James replied sitting in the chair that Naomi always sat in at the table.

"I don't understand." Abraham replied.

"I have had it, father. Naomi has been gone for way over a year and no one cares. None of the brethren have gone in search for her, nor have you. She is the only decent thing that has ever happened to our family and we have crapped on her."

"I did what I could to help her, James. I left her food on her doorstep and did what chores I could for her secretly."

"Have you ever asked yourself, father, why I am thirty years old and have never married?"

"I have wondered, but have been afraid to ask. If I had asked and found out you were a Sodom and Gomorrah man, you would have been shunned by our community. Some things are better left unsaid."

"I am not a homosexual. What I am is a man who has been in love with his brother's wife since the day she stepped off a bus in the city when she was sixteen. Had you and mother not rushed her into a two day courtship and then marriage to Joel, I might have had time to win her heart and her Adam and baby Mary would be mine and alive. Joel married her, but he did not love her. I knew from the moment I laid eyes on her that I was in love with her. You and mother, in your rush to give Joel respectability, did not allow Naomi and me to discover each other."

Abraham Toombs, in shock, plopped down in one of the kitchen chairs and began to laugh uncontrollably from stress. When he was done he looked at his son. "Naomi and her bread and butter kept me from going crazy the ten years she was with us. Do you know what it is like to be married to a woman you haven't slept with in twenty eight years and have not slept with anyone else? Naomi was the only light in my world. Your mother and I fell out of love twenty-eight years ago. Only our Amish tenets bind us together. Naomi is too young for me. However, had I not been married to your mother, I could have easily fallen in love with her."

"Don't let mother hear you say that. She is on a crusade to destroy Naomi. Father you have to know that mother is crazy, just like Joel? I also know that you have slept in a separate bed from her for all the years after her conception of Joel. I also understand that a man has needs. I myself am thirty and have suffered from the want of a woman's body. I need to know something. Mother secretly insists to me that Naomi's two children are yours. Are they father? I need to know. You have just said she was the light in your world."

"Naomi's children are Joel's. I have never done anything more than eat a piece of bread with cow's cream butter on it from Naomi. I have never touched her except for the day I found her in her kitchen floor bleeding to death. I had to rip her skirt off to see where the bleeding was coming from to try to save her. The brethren helped me. She was bleeding out and dying."

"Will you swear that on the Holy Bible, father?" James asked.

"Yes, James, I will. I have never touched Naomi. Adam and Mary belonged to Joel."

"I intend to find Naomi and bring her home, father. I have given it much consideration. I don't care if she is my brother's wife, I am going to help her get a divorce and marry her if she will have me. If the community shuns me, they will just have to do it. I should have gone after her over a year ago when she walked away from us. Only my respect, for you and mother, has kept me from doing so. I know how fragile my mother's thinking is and that she is about to go over the edge and snap. However, I am tired of mother calling Naomi a witch and I am tired of waiting to hear from Naomi. To be honest, I love Naomi more than I love the two of you."

"It is too late James. She is gone for good and there has been no communication from her. You can't find someone who doesn't want to be found. She has not put in a change of address with the postman. I have checked with him on a regular basis."

"She is not gone from my heart." James replied.

"This may surprise you James. I have kept it a secret because I have not wanted to get your mother's hopes up. I hired a detective, one of our former brethren, and your brother Joel has been found. He is not crazy, nor does he have amnesia. He has an illegal wife in Kentucky named Karen and a common law wife in Tennessee named Angela. They do not know about Naomi. Our Naomi had every right to sue Joel for a divorce on the grounds of adultery when she got out of the hospital six or so years ago. He married the woman named Karen just three to five weeks after marrying Naomi. His wanderings were his way of going home to her. He was not mentally mad. He was an adulterer with a second wife. Go up to the house and look at the items of Joel's that your mother and I found on the back of Joel's property hidden in a tree. He purposely kicked and tried to murder Naomi and her baby the day he left. Your mother is at the point of a nervous breakdown over what we have found. This is not a good time for you to leave here and go chasing after Naomi."

"I am going to kill Joel." James stated rising from the table. "Naomi almost died because of him and he wasn't even crazy."

Speechless, James left heading for his mother's house to look at the items found of Joel's.

Meanwhile in the kitchen of Naomi's farm house, Osceola Black Lightning did a little swish and sway with her long nail file making herself visible in the kitchen. She sat down where James had sat. Frankie Frances stood by her wondering why Ms. Osceola Black Lightning had made them visible to the adulterous farmer hick. Abraham had his face buried in his hands. Osceola did another little swish and closed Abraham's ears seeing that her motor mouth young assistant's volcano of a mouth was about to boil over with lava breath.

"What in the heck are we doing in this dust laden, deserted kitchen?" Frankie Frances asked putting her hand over her mouth to silence a cough. The room reeked with stale air.

"I am putting in a little overtime. I can work more than one case at once, if

I want. The sooner I make it thru the list of women that God has sent me to help, the sooner I get two days with my long legged Jack Rabbit."

"This is on our assignment list?' Frankie Frances asked eyeing the dusty kitchen and the older Amish man sitting in it. "Is he the reason we are breathing this stale air and viewing that blood stain over by the kitchen door? It looks like some country hick butchered a hog inside of this house. That monstrous stain over by the door speaks death."

"The blood stain is from Naomi. That is where Joel and his mother kicked her almost to death. That is where she lay dying and her unborn child convulsing."

Frankie Frances' eyes filled with tears. "That is why she sleeps in a locked closet! She is afraid he will return to kick her again."

"Yes, Frankie. Her husband almost killed her and did it on purpose with the toe of his boot. After Naomi lay unconscious, his mother also kicked her trying to finish her off."

"But why are we here? Naomi is back in Paducah." Frankie Frances stated eyeing the blood stain.

"I am marking one of my minor assignments off of my white cap mission list. It is Naomi's mother-in-law Martha that we have been assigned to put the mark of death on. She will not live much longer. Her time is about up. We are delivering to her the kiss of death. Only her husband's love will turn her from her darkness. He caused her darkness."

"But she got Naomi shunned insisting she was a witch and she kicked her. You just told me she did so. Why would we bother with her?"

"She lost her way, due to him. He did not believe her when she needed him to. He started her down the dark path to who she is now. She is a lost soul, hell bent on vengeance." Osceola replied in her syrupy voice. "She has broken just about every one of the Ten Commandments, but he is the cause."

"Why are we here and not in her kitchen a quarter mile down the road?"

"Every problem has a root, Frankie Frances, and in her case it is her husband. She sees him as having failed her when she needed him. She sees herself as unloved by him and has done everything in her power to keep him from leaving her. She actually loves him. He committed adultery once. Now she sees him doing it with every woman's face he innocently glances at. He accuses her of being an adulterer and she accuses him of the same. Both believe they are right. She doesn't see her vindictiveness and he doesn't see that he was wrong in not taking her side the day the woman with the gun walked her home."

"God isn't sticking me with an insensitive man to marry. That makes me a little smarter than you, Ms. Osceola Black Lightning. Someday, I will carry the nail file sword and you will be my assistant. You let the white suit tell you what to do and that includes who to marry. I embrace free-will choice. That makes me a little one up on you."

"We are angels, Frankie Frances. We don't have free will choice like the humans. We take what God gives us."

"Haven't you ever heard of returns, Ms. Osceola Black Lightning? If it doesn't fit, take it back. If God pairs me with some farm hick, back woods angel, I will say no thanks and return him."

"I heard that . . . !" A loud male's voice boomed followed by the sound of lightning cracking and thunder rolling.

Frankie Frances jumped and ducked behind the kitchen chair Osceola was seated in, hoping the White Suit didn't punish her by giving her more pimples.

Osceola broke out into belly laughter knowing her assistant was hiding from the White Suit. When she could control her laughter, she stated. "Well, at least you know he is listening to you today." Then she looked up to Heaven, grinned, and threw God a kiss on the end of her fingers.

The lightning and thunder caught Abraham Toombs' attention and he removed his face from his hands. "Where is that coming from?" He asked in a mutter. "There isn't a hint of a cloud in the sky today."

Then, he turned his attention to the table and jumped up in shock. A huge, black woman was sitting across from him at Naomi's table drinking water from a fruit jar. A half eaten fruit jar of peaches set in front of her with a spoon resting on the Jar's lid.

"Who are you and why are you in this kitchen?" He demanded. Then he spotted a smaller, white female standing behind the huge black woman pushing eye glasses up her nose like they had slid down due to her nose being greased with hog fat.

Osceola stood. "I am Osceola Black Lightning, God's number one death angel."

"You are what?" Abraham smirked. "You do not have wings. Now tell me who you are and why you have broken into this house."

Frankie Frances, feeling Osceola needed her protection, stepped around the table's end and planted her feet about sixteen inches apart in preparation to do battle. He was no match for her. She was used to wrestling and leashing the hounds of Heaven.

"Back off you bearded, zipper-less, country hick. Mess with her and you might get by with it, but you don't want to mess with me. I am Frankie Frances Periwinkle, Heaven's number one dog walker and I could leash you and tie you out back to a porch post with one swish of my wrist. Believe me; you don't want to mess with me. God even gets out of my way, when he sees me coming. You want wings, watch this."

Frankie Frances turned and looked at Osceola with a toothy grin from ear to ear asking in her honey dipped give me a chance voice, "May I just use your nail file sword just this once. I just want to show this country hick what real wings are. He is used to goose feather pillows and fried chicken wings."

Osceola grinned and replied in her syrupy, sticky sweet voice. "You may use it, just this once! You are grounded from your sword, in case you don't remember."

Frankie Frances took the fourteen inch long nail file and held it at eye level. She bit her lip and gave it a little swish and sway. Instantly she had wings that stood three feet above her head. The ends of the wings brushed the floor like the trail on a wedding gown. Then she swished and swayed Osceola's nail file sword again adorning Osceola with huge, white, monstrous wings that touched the ceiling of the room. Osceola, now standing, grinned and stretched her wings which spanned the width of the kitchen, to please Frankie Frances. She then did a little dance number, referred to as the Dance of Love, across the kitchen floor, pretending that her long legged Jack Rabbit was in her harms. Frankie Frances gave a little swish of her nail file sword and there was instant music for Osceola to dip and sway to.

"What dance was that?" Frankie Frances asked when Osceola finished. She had never seen her show any passion before. Osceola had moves.

"It is the Dance of Lovers who has not seen each other for a while. I plan to do it with my long legged Jack Rabbit when I see him again." Osceola replied in her syrupy, sticky, voice. For the moment, she was ignoring the big eyed Amish man who was trembling in his work boots. It wasn't often, lately, that she got to strut her stuff. White caps weren't a dancing culture.

"Oh my God . . . have you come for me?" Abraham asked falling on his knees and clutching his heart. "I did strut and dance with the Molly woman twenty- eight years ago. She taught me the Dance of Love. I now repent of that sin."

"Get up from there," Osceola stated. "And show me what you got."

Abraham Toombs stood to his feet. Osceola Black Lightning grabbed one of his hands and forced it around her waist and then took his other in hers and extended it preparing to dance. The love dance began to play as Frankie Frances once more started the music by swishing her nail file sword. In shock, Abraham Toombs began to move with her. Osceola had a way with men. She could swish and sway and they always followed. His shocked expression then turned to one of pure enjoyment as they moved about Naomi's kitchen doing the love dance. When the music ended, he dipped Osceola low like Molly had taught him so many years before. For a moment he was young and in love again.

"You are pretty good." Osceola stated letting him go. "I will return for a dance now and then. I think I just might let you live to see a few more days. It is hard to find a good dance partner."

"Dancing is a . . . is a sin!" He spit out in spite of the fact that he had just walked down memory lane and re-experienced what it had been like to be in Molly's arms, the woman that he had an affair with and had fallen in love with. He had always denied loving her to Martha.

"Lighten up, Abraham. God put you down here to live life, not run from it. Have you ever thought about grabbing your wife, Martha, and moving her around her kitchen? Your marriage just might improve. It is never too late to fall in love with a woman again. A man, who doesn't strut his stuff, sleeps alone."

"I couldn't do that. It would be disrespectful to Molly." He blurted out and then bit his lip realizing what he had said.

"Married to a woman you think is a Devil and in love with a memory. That will get you know where." Osceola shot back. "You did make a choice many years ago, and it wasn't Molly. God expects you to honor your choice, your wife. The White Suit has seen your secret winks at Molly over the years. They are adultery of the heart. You say you have chosen your wife, but in your heart you have not. Secret sinners are not going to get the royal treatment up there. You are a liar, Abraham Toombs. I believe the Good Book says 'Thou shall not lie!"

"You have indeed pointed out my secret sins. I will wink at Molly no more and stand by my choice."

"You will do more than stand by your choice. You will make amends with Martha." Osceola stated loudly.

Osceola then took her nail file from Frankie Frances and swished and swayed it till the whole back wall of the kitchen behind her turned into one huge, metal gate to Hell. Flames danced behind it and demons rattled the bars of the gate trying to escape the flames. Once again, Abraham fell to his knees trembling in fear.

"I repent of not sleeping with my wife and keeping my commitment. I repent of falling in love with my daughter-in-law Naomi. I repent of anything that I have failed to remember to repent of. Please don't open that gate and throw me in there. I repent angel. I have indeed held to the memories of Molly. I will do whatever you say including waltzing Martha around her kitchen. I will make amends."

"Does he sound sincere?" Osceola asked in her syrupy, sticky voice turning to Frankie Frances who had her mouth wide open staring at the gate. She had never seen Hell's Gate before; she was trembling.

"I don't know about him, but I now repent of a secret sin, Ms. Osceola Black Lightning. I ate more than my half of that jar of peaches from Naomi's pantry that we opened. I am a glutton!"

Osceola grinned at her assistant and bit her lip for a moment to keep from laughing. She had purposely not eaten her half, so the kid could have most of them.

"One small pimple coming up, Frankie Frances. I think that should be sufficient punishment for all of that sugar. You won't go to Hell, today."

"What about me?" Abraham asked as he knelt on the floor, eyeing the dancing flames and the demons who were screeching at ear piercing sound levels.

"God heard your words that you do not wish to die old and alone. Disaster is about to call on your family, Abraham Toombs. You are to stand by your choice. Also, you are to stand by Naomi, not your son Joel. Your daughter is one of God's friends. Your son with the kicking boot is like the demons behind the gate. He is not one of God's. He is a dark soul who stole a human body before a white soul was placed in it. When you are old and Martha is gone, you are to make your way to Naomi and live in the land of the English with her." Osceola stated in her syrupy, sticky, fly swatting voice.

"I hear you, angel." He replied with perspiration beads running down his face. Then there was a moment of silence while Osceola caused her wings to move making everything in the kitchen that was on shelves to fly about the room. Then she folded her wings away.

"You are good!" Frankie Frances stated eyeing Osceola and then the gate of Hell which was starting to fade.

"I am the Death Angel, known in Heaven as Osceola Black Lightning. You Abraham Toombs will mend your ways with your wife Martha. Fail to do so, and I will return and take the breath from all of your livestock, the fish in your pond, the birds flying over your house, your wife, your son James, and everything that ever crawls, walks, and moves in your presence. We are Naomi's guardians. Your wife was once as sweet as Naomi. You did not listen to her the day she tried to tell you she was taken by the English man and almost raped. You believed the worst of her. You will pay for the dark path she has walked down. You caused it. Her sins lay at your feet."

Frankie Frances nudged Osceola and spread her feet apart and fluttered her wings. "I am Frankie Frances Periwinkle, angel and walker of the hounds of Heaven. You think the demons behind the gate are scary, just mess with me. I will cause your nose and ears to have so many hairs in them that you can't sniff or hear the call of your master. This is just a little reminder of what I can do to you." She stated twirling one of her dog leashes. It then fell around Abraham's neck and she started pulling him toward the gate of hell intending to tie him to its front gate like she did the hounds of Heaven. He started to fight the leash and held to anything he could get a hold of as she dragged him toward the dancing flames and demons with their arms stretched out thru the bars trying to grab him. He screamed, and begged for mercy. Frankie Frances then handed her end of the dog leash to one of the demons who started to draw Abraham to him.

"Please angel, save me, I will do anything you say. Please dog walker, I will be a good hound, I promise." Abraham screamed and begged for mercy as he was about to be overcome by the demons strength on the other end of his leash.

"You will do anything I say?" Frankie Frances asked grinning at Osceola.

"Anything . . . , I will swear on God's Holy Bible." Abraham quickly yelled as the demon had him with in an arm's length.

"Okay . . ." Frankie Frances stated taking back the handle to the leash from the demon. She then removed the leash from around Abraham's neck and he ran across the kitchen and flattened himself against the far wall in fear of the angels and the demons. He was trembling and had wet his trousers. He slid down the wall to a knelt position because his legs had become like jelly he was so afraid.

"Fix your marriage, Abraham Toombs! Your wife will not live long and she is assigned to me. I want her to take a reverse walk on the dark path she is on. I want her turned toward the light and walking in that direction. Do you understand?" Osceola Black Lightning boomed in a loud, demanding, syrupy, sticky, fly swatting voice as beads of perspiration ran down Abraham's face. She loved making men tremble and sweat. Women always got the short end of the stick in Earth life. Making a man bow, here and there, brought her great pleasure.

"I will fix my marriage and be faithful to my wife. I will waltz her around her kitchen and do the Dance of Love with her." He replied wringing wet with sweat and collapsed on his knees.

"Rise, you dancing fool, and get out of here before I set your dancing shoes on fire with a flame that you will never be able to put out." Osceola demanded.

Frankie Frances muttered to herself, "Athlete's Foot. I never thought about that one."

Instantly, Abraham jumped up and ran from Naomi's house and then straight home as fast as he could sprint to see if his wife and son James were okay. Then he checked out his livestock. There was a small fire burning outside of his barn doors about the size of a campfire. He grabbed a bucket hanging beside his bags of feed and started bucketing water from an outside water trough trying to put the small fire out. He could not put it out. He knew instantly that the angel intended to start by burning his barn down if he didn't do as he was told. Dropping the bucket, he ran for his farmhouse with his hat blowing off. He didn't stop to retrieve it. Sprinting up his back steps two at a time, he threw his kitchen door open and stepped inside in a panic. Martha was heating water in a kettle to wash the five years of dirt from Joel's found clothing. Abraham grabbed his wife by the shoulders, spun her around, took her in his arms and kissed her passionately like he had never kissed her before. Then he picked her up so her feet were not touching her kitchen floor and did the Dance of Love moving her around their kitchen. He did not sleep alone that night. He slept in her bed and made sure she was satisfied. It is amazing what a little visitation from a death angel and her assistant can accomplish.

Frankie Frances and Osceola returned to Paducah to resume their boring duty of guarding Naomi and having their usual chats on the third floor landing to pass the time in the invisible.

"Didn't you put it on a little thick with the words you spoke to Abraham?" Frankie Frances asked as Osceola did a little swish and sway to detour a skunk that was about to take up residence below the stairs. She didn't want Naomi's nose to be affected by the skunk's odor. She was guarding her.

"Men always expect angels to be a little dramatic. They want to tremble and wet their trousers when they see one. Humans like to be frightened and then laugh about it afterward. That is a good thing? Laughter is the best medicine." Osceola replied.

"What did you think about my wings?" Frankie Frances asked grinning from ear to ear.

"They were a little bit oversize, but they filled the bill. He wanted wings, he got them. Next time, make mine a little shorter. I almost tripped on them while I was dancing."

"You are never happy with me, Ms. Osceola Black Lightning. You should have put in your order a head of time, if you wanted short wings."

"I am putting in my order right now. Should the occasion arise again, I want shorter wings and definitely not white ones. They are too ordinary. I am a designer girl. Make mine diamond studded."

"Why do Earthlings always want us to appear with wings? They are cumbersome to wear, smelly, and take a lot of bleaching to keep them white. I hate my bleach loads when I do laundry. They are so stained and stinky. You know, Osceola, I think the next time I create us wings, I will design myself a royal purple pair and maybe a chartreuse pair for you. You are right! We are not the ordinary white robed, white winged type. Plus, we can throw them in with our colors, when we wash."

"I am definitely not ordinary." Osceola laughed in her syrupy voice. "However, I know what a dry cleaner is. Let them worry about the bleaching of my white wings and under things. I have better things to do."

"Damn it. I forgot something." Frankie Frances stated firmly in her honey dipped, young voice. She was clearly irritated with herself.

"Watch your language, Frankie Frances. God may not be listening to you at the moment, but I am. Now, what did you forget?"

"I should have made us hover in mid air, and then flew us around the room a couple of times."

"That room wasn't big enough for a dove to flap about in," Osceola replied, "Much less us."

"I hadn't thought about that. We were like birds in a cage, weren't we?" Frankie Frances retorted and then paused before adding, "The Amish should build their wives bigger, bird cage kitchens if they want visits from us."

CHAPTER EIGHT

Pack Your Things

Fall flew by and the last two weekends of the Farmer's market had arrived. Jack told Naomi that the big case he was working on was coming to a close. Also, he and Karen had somewhat became a couple. The incident with Jenkins and Adam Too seemed to be history. Marcus was looking forward to March when Naomi would be divorced and free to see him. He had not heard from his sister Angela in months. Naomi fantasized that Marcus would stand with her and not his sister when the time came. Her racing heart for him had not ceased.

All was peaceful amongst the four friends and each had their own hopes for the future. Marcus wanted Naomi. Karen wanted Jack. Jack wanted Naomi. Naomi wanted to be free to fall in love with Marcus. Lost in their naïve wants, none saw the coming storm that would end their friendships. There is always a lull before a storm. The four friends were living and breathing in that false sense of calm.

It was Friday afternoon and Naomi had an appointment with her attorney. His secretary had called and asked her to come in for an update on her case. Naomi once more made her way to Dan Maynard's office for an update. She entered his office and sat down in the familiar seat across from him and waited for him to shuffle a few papers around on his desk. He seemed lost in thought about something. She patiently waited for him to wade into whatever it was that he wished to speak to her about.

"Sorry . . ." Dan Maynard stated picking up a couple of photos. "I was taking a quick look at the latest detective findings in your case. I have a couple of new items to show you, and give you an update on our count- down to get Joel arrested for polygamy. I think you are going to be pleased. The arrest warrants are now being processed and his arrest will take place not tomorrow, but the following Saturday."

"He will be arrested on the last Saturday of the Farmer's Market season?" Naomi asked making sure she had not heard him wrong. Originally, he had told her it would be March.

"Yes, on that Saturday. Law enforcement from several states and the F.B.I. are involved. First on the list will be his arrest and then the serving of your divorce papers on the grounds of adultery and polygamy. With a polygamy charge against him, I am sure he won't fight you on the divorce, because he has no grounds. His only interest, on the designated Saturday, will probably be in trying to make bail and then disappear like he did on you. However, you will get a divorce whether he shows his face in court or not. I think I can possibly get you a divorce court date set in January."

"Oh . . . , that is wonderful. I have but a little over two months of silence left to put in."

"Pack your tote with what is important to you, Naomi. I will be telling you to vacate your apartment sometime in the next eight days. Joel's one illegal wife in St. Louis got suspicious and has kicked him out. He is currently residing with the second secret one he has stashed there. We are going with what we have before he runs and disappears to a wife we don't know about. We now have seven documented secret wives and families. My detective feels there may be another four or five out there. However, we don't want Joel disappearing on us. It is time for us to play our cards. When Joe is served his papers a week from tomorrow, Karen and all of the other wives will also be served with subpoenas to appear in court as divorce court witnesses in your case. If Joel somehow makes bail, I don't want you in that apartment. Karen is the only one of the women he seems to have feelings for. He may head straight for her trying to con her to let him hide him out possibly in her basement. He once had a studio down there."

"I will pack my tote tonight. The farmer's market season is basically over. I will just bake and take bread for my regular customers tomorrow. Then I will wash up all my pans and pack."

"Do you have a secret, safe place to flee to?"

"Yes, my friend Jack has given me the key to his apartment. I will go there first and from there catch a bus to Missouri and spend a few days with my friend, Rachael. After that, I will rent a room somewhere till my court date."

"You must rent a room in Kentucky till January. You must reside in the state you are suing for divorce in." He replied.

"I understand. After Rachael, I will make my way back here and rent myself a room a couple towns away and keep my silence."

"Here . . . !" He stated pushing a prepaid cell phone across the desk to her. "If this cell phone rings, it is a call from me telling you to vacate. Keep it charged and turned on day and night. There may not be time to send my secretary to tell you it is time. St. Louis and Nashville are within hours of here. I want you safe."

"I understand." Naomi replied nervous and excited at the same time. She was going to be free and sooner than she thought.

"There is one odd little detail that my detective discovered as he pursued your case."

"What is that, Mr. Maynard?"

"I was wrong about the prostitute in Nashville, Marcus' sister. According to her neighbors and her landlord, Joel is her common law husband and has been so for about five or six years. The landlord told my detective that he wanders in and out of her life just like he did you back on the farm. Your husband, Joel, has married all the women he has dated, except her. She does have three children that she claims belongs to him. However, his name is not on their birth certificates. His name is on those born to him in his seven polygamist marriages."

"So, Joel did name her children after my son and daughter and his mother."

"Apparently he did Naomi. He also named all of his other wives' children with the names Adam, Abraham, Mary, Martha, and James."

"He created himself a new family and gave them our names." Naomi replied in a sad voice.

"Yes, he did and just like you he abandoned all of the wives when he got what he wanted from them. He walked away letting them wonder what had happened to him."

"What is Marcus' sister like?"

"She is one ugly, obese woman who sucks the welfare system for her living. She is ugly as sin and has no money. Her lack of money may be the reason Joel has not married her. He does have a sociopath pattern of marrying beautiful, professional women who work or have inherited money. What I can tell you about her is that she met Joel when he abandoned you for good. His second wife Karen threw him out when she was a junior in college. He spent two what you call good years with you and then he headed for Kentucky to reunite with Karen. He met Marcus' sister on his way to Kentucky. He had money on him at the time. Miss Bates was a high school dropout who ran away with him. He stashed her in a cheap room in Nashville paying for two nights rent and then abandoned her heading for Kentucky. After the two nights with the run-away, she got pregnant. The girl, Marcus' sister, worked the streets for a while to feed herself. After the baby came, she milked the welfare system and has been doing so ever since. She gives most of the money she makes on the side as a prostitute to Joel when he pops in on her. She does not know about you, Karen, or his other multiple wives and children. He uses her for whatever he can get out of her. She uses Marcus for whatever she can get out of him. She is a gutter rat."

"That dooms my friendship with Marcus. I do not want bastard, carbon copies of my dead son Adam and my murdered daughter Mary as part of my new life. I will not disrespect my two dead children by embracing them. I will enjoy my last Saturday at the market friendship with him tomorrow, but be prepared to walk away when you ring this cell phone. My children deserve to know that when the chips were down, I stood unwavering with them. I will not stand with the wives and children who in a roundabout manner caused the death of my children."

"I understand, Naomi. However, keep your opinions to yourself till after we bring him to justice. Any of the wives that we can get to testify willingly, is to our advantage."

"I understand, Mr. Maynard. I will remain silent, continue my life as it is for the next seven or eight days, and not rock my boat. I want a divorce and justice for my children."

"Remember, keep the cell phone on and in your pocket at all times. When your husband is arrested for polygamy and served with divorce papers from you, all Hell is going to break loose. Karen Cameron, your landlord, will see you as having befriended her to obtain information for your own divorce case. She will not be a happy camper and possibly try to assault you. You have to keep in mind Naomi, Karen is a drunk and drunks do strange things including pulling out guns and other weapons that normally they would only use if they were broken in on. Leave immediately when I call you. You will have an hour maybe before Karen is served."

"I understand. I will keep the phone on and my rolling tote packed with whatever is important to me."

"It is possible that you will be a free woman the first week in January." Dan Maynard stated pausing for a moment. "Naomi, I want to caution you as to how violent Joel is. A behavioral science F.B.I. friend of mind has told me that your Joel is just one step away from starting to murder the wives he abandons for whatever assets they have. There is a woman missing in Iowa just above St. Louis who has three children who are named Mary, Adam, and Abraham. She is feared dead and the F.B.I. is working round the clock to tie that case to your husband. She came up missing about six months ago. In my thinking, Naomi, your Joel has crossed the line and is capable of doing anything at this point."

"He tried to kick me and my baby to death. He succeeded with my baby, Mary. He crossed the line back then, Mr. Maynard. He may have kicked many besides me since. I saw the darkness in his eyes the day he tried to kill me."

Standing in the invisible shadows of the office, Frankie Frances and Osceola stood listening.

"Do you know what, Ms. Osceola Black Lightning?" Frankie Frances asked frowning.

"What . . . , Frankie Frances?" She answered watching Naomi rise to leave.

"We should fly to St. Louis and take your sword and cut off all the toes of that kicking Joel. Then we should take his toes and wave our nail file and make them kick him till there was nothing left of him or them."

"We are not angels of vengeance, Frankie Frances. Our mission is to guard Naomi. We are guardians, in case you have forgotten. I am sure the angel of vengeance will do her thing. However, your idea of turning his toes on him is a good one."

"I am good. Maybe I should set my goal to be an angel of vengeance instead of a guardian." Frankie Frances replied in her honey dipped, young, southern voice.

"Well, don't get to enthusiastic about a new goal. I said your idea was a good one. I didn't say it was the best one."

"You are picking on me again. Spit it out! What would you do to Naomi's husband if you were an angel of vengeance?"

"Number one, he likes women. I would take my sword and cut off his male thing. That would end his loving days. Next, I would blind him. If he can't see a pretty woman, he can't con one. Third, I would cut out his tongue so he couldn't sweet talk a woman. Tongue-less, thing-less, and blind would put a stop to his deceptions. A blind man cannot wander, a thing-less man cannot make love, and a tongue less man cannot entice a woman with his words. I would then leave the kicking and killing of the sucker up to God. He has big boots."

"You just love sweeping me under the rug, Ms. Osceola Black Lightning. You just love to try to outdo me. Does it make you feel big and powerful to put me down? People like you pick on the weaker like me to make themselves look big. I have got your number and I am going to tell God on you when I get home. You are trying to destroy my self esteem."

"I would like to destroy more than your self esteem, Frankie Frances. I am just waiting for God to give me permission." Osceola replied irritated.

CHAPTER NINE

Angela's Wedding Announcement

Two Saturdays remained of the market season. The first was a very cold day and the coffee that Marcus and Naomi had shared was long gone. Both of them were rubbing their arms between customers trying to stay warm.

"Would you like some hot chocolate?" He asked Naomi after a customer left his booth. I am about to freeze. We could sit in my jeep and drink it, if you would like. The customers are scarce this morning and the season is basically over.

"Some hot chocolate would be very nice, but I cannot sit with you in your jeep and you know why." Naomi replied. "However, I have something I wish to say to you. Next Saturday may not come for us and I wish to make the most of today."

"What is it?" He asked.

"Do you remember all the times you have asked me to walk down by the river with you?"

"Yes, I remember every one of them and also your turn downs. Looking back now, I know why you turned me down. You were watching your backside because of your impending divorce."

"Yes, that was the reason. The season is over Marcus and my attorney tells me that I possibly have a divorce court date the first week in January. I am really excited. Before, he had told me it would be March."

"That is the best news I have had all season." He replied smiling. "Two months and you are my girl."

"Jack has asked me to have a hamburger downtown with him this evening at five. He wishes to speak with me about something. I think perhaps he might be considering a ring for Karen and wishes me to take a peek at the downtown jeweler. Afterward, if you are willing, I will take that walk down by the river with you. I may not see you after today, till possibly January. The last day of the market I will not be here. I am going to a wedding. I want to have a moment with you tonight alone and tell you that I love you."

"Oh my God . . . you said it. You said you love me!" He muttered in shock.

"How could I not love you? Will you meet me at my place at six? We will walk downtown and then to the river. I still cannot sit with you in your jeep without a chaperone."

"Naomi, you have just made me the happiest man on the face of this planet. I will be at your place six sharp. I love you too. More, than you will ever know."

"Do not be late tonight, Marcus. This is important to me." Naomi stated turning to wait on a customer who was interested in one of her pans of corn bread.

Marcus left his booth to walk down to the snack shack vendor for two cups of hot chocolate. He was one happy man. He whistled as he walked. Then his cell phone rang. He flipped his phone open and saw that it was Angela's number. He cringed and thought about not answering it. However, if it was important, he would never forgive himself. She had threatened to kill her children the last time she called.

"Hello . . ." Marcus answered reluctantly.

"You are a little slow on the pickup; brother . . . did I catch you in bed with Jenkins?"

"I have not seen Jenkins in months. I have someone new in my life and no I am not in bed with her this time of the day. It is going on noon, Angela. What do you want?" He retorted in an irritated voice. Jenkins was a sore subject between him and Naomi and he did not want to be caught talking on the cell phone about her.

"Clear your evening and pick me and the kids up at the bus station at five. I have something exciting to tell you."

"I have a date at six, Angela. I am not going to be at home." He retorted thinking of his long awaited walk down by the river with Naomi. He had waited for over a year for her to agree to something as simple as a walk down by the river with him. In a way, it was like prom night, that big chance to finally take the most beautiful girl in the world to a dance and then be alone with her. He felt like a seventeen year old looking forward to the walk.

"Well, break it and don't be late picking me and the kids up. I have something to tell you and I want to do it in person. Also, I need you to take the kids for a week."

"I am not taking the kids. You find someone else. I have a lady friend and we have plans."

"Adam has told me about your ugly, bottom of the education barrel, bread maker at the market. What happened to that pompous ass brother of mine who dated only professional women with master degrees? Are you suddenly into slum dating?"

"I have grown up, Angela. If it is any of your business, I am dating a holiness woman like mom."

"That is a shocker!" Angela retorted. "You better wake up and dump her before she throws your wine cooler out as well as the lingerie from your last four paying lovers!"

"This woman is the one, Angela. I plan on marrying her as soon as I can convince her to do so. The bachelor magazines, lingerie, wine cooler, and the beer are already out of my house and at my doing, not hers. If you ever mention any of my previous girlfriends to her, I will cut you and your kids totally off. She is that special someone that only comes along once in a lifetime. As much as I love you and your kids, when I marry her, she becomes first with me."

"Get over it, Marcus. Six months and you will move on to someone else or it will be Jenkins again. How many times have you had an affair with the married, blonde bimbo? My last count was three. You always run back to her."

"Not this time, Angela. I have found my soul mate and I have no desire to ever look at another woman again. I wish I had never dated Jenkins or the other women. I should have waited for my bread maker to come along. Mom was right when she was telling us to wait for the right one to come along. I am garbage next to my bread maker."

"Well, my right one did come along and you and our parents have never accepted him." She retorted in a huff.

"Joe does not love you, Angela. If he did he would have married you years ago and got you off the streets. He pimps you."

"Our parents put us thru teenage hell making us dress and speak according to their cult's holiness rules. Our parent's are crazies, in case you have forgotten." She shot back.

"Our parents may have been a little overly strict, Angela, but they are not crazy. Our mother is a decent woman who lives what she believes."

"Good old mom didn't pick on you, like she did me. I was the black sheep in the family, the evil one." His sister whined and then changed the subject seeing she was getting nowhere with him. "The kids are looking forward to a few days with you. Dump your bread maker and be at the bus station or I will waltz over to your house and leave the kids with one of your neighbors and walk away. I don't care which one. I will take them up to the door, ring the bell, leave them, and let you do the explaining."

"Don't you do that, Angela! I have worked hard for my respected position in my neighborhood."

"Well then, pick me up at the station. You know I do what I say."

"What is so damn important that you are wanting to ruin my life over?" He asked in a mad tone knowing that he was once more getting dumped on.

"I will tell you when I get there.

"Do not bring the kids, Angela. I am serious about my lady friend and I have a serious date with her this evening."

"And just who do you expect me to leave them with? I am not exactly bosom buddies with anyone. They are coming."

"Ask mom to take them! I have a full teaching schedule as well as being in the middle of writing my book on gourds. The woman I am seeing is a no nonsense woman like mom. I can't ask her to include your kids in our budding relationship."

"Lighten up, Marcus. There is more than one bread baking, plain Jane out there. Besides, I have something important to tell you."

"Can't you just tell me over the phone?" He asked trying to get around a visit from her as well as her dumping the kids on him.

"I will see you at five. The kids can eat whatever. Throw them some peanut butter on a spoon. They will be happy with it. Pick me up one of those catfish and barbecue bean plate dinners from the bistro." She stated and hung up before he could reply.

"Damn it . . . damn it . . . damn it . . . ! For the first time in months, things are going right in my world. Now Angela is going to dump her kids on me again. Where am I going to find a baby sitter for tonight?" He muttered totally pissed.

After paying for some hot chocolate he returned to the booths and stood sipping his with Naomi.

"Our walk at six is very important to me, Marcus. You may park in front of my apartment and we will start our walk there and then thru the business district and end up down by the river. Do not be late. I have words to say to you that I have spent much time thinking about. Tonight is very important to me."

"I will be there with bells on." Marcus replied and then added. "I may be five or ten minutes late. I have a plumber coming to work on a stopped up sink at five." He said fishing for some reason to not to have to explain Angela's sudden visit and intrusion on their time. It was just a little white lie that he didn't think mattered and he might need the extra ten minutes to pick up a teen baby sitter somewhere. He would give Angela some cash and she could catch a cab back to the bus station.

"Remember, I am having a hamburger with Jack at five? He asked me earlier. I think he wants me to possibly help him pick out a birthday gift for Karen, possibly a ring. Her birthday is next week. He bought me this pin to thank me for nursing him last winter." She stated pointing to a gold safety pin that she had her money pocket secured with.

Marcus grinned. "It sounds like old Jack is about to surrender his bachelor-hood to Karen, just like me."

"And just why would you be surrendering your bachelor hood? I don't recall you asking anyone to marry you." She smirked.

"I have every intention of kneeling on one knee and putting an engagement ring on your finger, just as soon as you are divorced. Consider yourself pre-asked." He laughed.

"Tonight, Marcus. It is important to me." She replied once more and then turned to wait on another customer. She knew it would be her final goodbye to him, although he might not know it. After her divorce she would be moving on. Deep down she knew he would stand with his sister and not her when her agenda of getting Joel arrested for polygamy was discovered. She wanted this last evening with him so that she would have a good memory of them to take with her.

As she waited on a couple of customers, she thought how wonderful her new shoes felt. Jack had showed up with them on Thursday evening saying they were an early Christmas present. She knew it was his way of taking care of her. She could read him like a book. He was always seeing to her everyday needs and standing behind her when the chips were down. Last Thursday he had brought her a can of cinnamon. She was indeed out in her cupboard. He always seemed to sense what she needed or was out of including lady products which he showed up with occasionally telling her he had found them on sale. She felt safe with him and could trust him. Her friend, Karen, was lucky to have such a wonderful, kind, thoughtful man in her life.

In the invisible, Frankie Frances turned to Osceola as they stood behind Naomi in her booth.

"She should just run away with Marcus and live for the moment; to heck with his sister." Frankie Frances stated pushing her glasses up her nose.

"What if he is not the one for her, Frankie Frances? If you run off with someone who possibly isn't the one, you mess up your whole life." Osceola replied in her sticky, syrupy voice, as she filed her nails.

"Well, just because you run off doesn't mean you can't come back. Mrs. God's hounds of Heaven are always running off. They come home when they get hungry. If I was Naomi, I would run off with him, use him up, and then come home when Heaven's dinner bell rings."

"A man with a dog mentality is not worth having." Osceola replied. "They run off and bring home fleas, mud that they have rolled in, and dirty paws that have been everywhere. Only a dog would run off with a dog."

"You just called me a dog, Ms. Osceola Black Lightning. That was not nice. I may be a dog walker, but I am not a dog."

"You couldn't prove that by me. You just said that you would like to run off with Marcus, use him up, and then make it home for dinner. If you have a dog mentality, you are a dog." She replied.

"When I get back to heaven, I am going to tell God you called me a dog. He will probably let me leash you, march you up to the gate of Hell, and then kick your backside into Hell's fiery cage."

"The last time I talked to God, he told me that you didn't walk his dogs, they walked you. If you have a leash around your neck, you are a dog."

"You just wait . . . I will get even with you for calling me a dog. You just wait and see. Once day I will grow up and be the biggest and best angel dog walker in all of Heaven. I will kick your old backside into my dog catcher truck and send you off to the pound where you might or might not get fed. Then I will find your long legged Jack Rabbit man and throw him in my dog catcher truck. I will make Rabbit stew out of him and feed him to all the dogs in the pound and let you watch." Frankie Frances replied mad.

"You can try anything you want with me, Frankie Frances, but you go messing with my Jack Rabbit and I will break your glasses, pull every hair out of your ponytail, pull all of your teeth, break your ten fingers and then your ten toes, and crochet your dog leashes into a rug. Do you get what I am saying?" Osceola asked in her syrupy, sticky, fly swatting voice.

"Just wait till I tell God on you, Ms. Osceola Black Lightning. He is going to charge you with mental child abuse. You just threatened to physically harm me. I am just thirteen. I wasn't doing a thing to you and you just verbally assaulted me."

"See that little white truck type van coming up the street?" Osceola asked in her syrupy voice.

"Yes . . . why are you asking?" Frankie Frances inquired as she pushed her glasses up her nose so she could see what type of truck it was.

"Just tell me what kind of a truck it is."

"It is a truck from the city's dog pound why." Frankie Frances asked.

Osceola who had been filing her nails quickly gave a little swish and a sway with her nail file sword and instantly, Frankie Frances was in the middle of the street below and Osceola had turned her into a barking little ankle nipper. The pound truck stopped and the driver got out. When Frankie Frances, now a little Chihuahua, was nipping at the man's ankles, he snatched her up by the neck and threw her in the back of the pound truck and slammed the door on her.

"I am good!" Osceola stated grinning. "I will go get her out of the pound tomorrow after she has had her shots and eaten puppy food for three meals."

Then a booming voice called. "O . . . s . . . c . . . e . . . o . . . l . . . a . . . !"

"Yes . . . God . . ." She answered quickly in her syrupy voice expecting to be chastised for turning her assistant into a dog and then caging her.

"Good Job. I wish I had thought of that one!"

CHAPTER TEN

A Burger with Jack

I t had been an extremely busy day. After returning from her last day at the farmer's market, Naomi washed up all of her baking pans and packed her pulling tote with what was important to her. She then stepped into the shower to freshen up for her outing for a hamburger with jack. As the water cascaded over her, she gave thanks for the simple pleasure of indoor water and her shower. She would miss her apartment and its amenities when she had to move on in less than a week. Back on the farm she had to carry a bucket of water and then heat it on her wood stove to bathe in. Life had been pleasant in her bird nest on the third floor. She did not know what pleasantness or unpleasantness lay ahead of her after next Saturday. So now she felt a need to tell each of her friends how much she cared about them, even if they turned on her later. It was the moment in which she lived that was important. She had held them all at arm's length. Now, it was time to embrace them and silently tell them goodbye. She would not be able to do so later. Her time in Paducah was up. Dan Maynard would call before the week was up telling her to leave.

Stepping from her shower, she dried and put on a fresh dress and then a white cap after brushing her hair. She looked in the mirror and saw older eyes looking at her than what she remembered. She was fifteen going on sixteen when she married Joel. Now she was sliding down the hill toward thirty. She was not a young girl wondering where her husband had wandered off to while she breast fed a newborn son and tried to keep up with his chores. She was now a grown woman who knew to question when a man said he loved you, to question everything and make decisions that were right for her.

She looked in the mirror at the dark circles around her eyes, the result of too many lonely, sleepless nights waiting for her husband to be brought to justice. Now the ending of her nightmare was in sight. When she left in a few days on a bus for Missouri, she would kiss her life in Paducah goodbye. Her friends would just be memories. She had been careful not to accumulate things. Her baking pans had come from garage sales. They could be left behind and easily replaced down the road at more garage sales wherever she ended up after the wedding she would attend with Rachael. Her new wedding quilt she would leave with jack. He deserved the best she had to give. He had never failed to be there for her. She would once more travel light, wearing as many clothes as she could possibly walk in comfortably and carry a tote with her sewing supplies, female products, her bible, and a starter for sourdough bread in a pint fruit jar. She would carry her money in her pocket pinned tightly with the gold safety pin that Jack had bought her. Next to her Bible, it was her most prized possession.

Joel had taken everything from her. She had denied herself all pleasures including Marcus in order to bring Joel to justice. All the money she had made baking bread had been spent on an attorney to divorce him. He had stripped her clean. However, for the first time in years she could see light at the end of her dark tunnel. The next time she started over she would be free to love and be a woman again. She would also be free to create a world for herself that was hers. She would be all she could be and if a man wanted to be with her, he would have to live in her world, not her in his. She would be like Molly. She would not be disrespected ever again. She would rule her new world and her new life.

Looking at herself in the mirror, she realized that she had not secured her pocket. She put a few dollars in it and then pinned it closed with the wonderful gold safety pin that Jack had given her. He would be the hardest to tell goodbye. He was her rock and right arm. She not only wanted to tell Marcus how much she loved and appreciated him, she also wanted to tell Jack. Her words would mean nothing once they all turned on her and they saw her as a vengeful woman who had used them to gather information. She knew that God had orchestrated the whole event of her traveling to Paducah. Each person she had met along the way was a piece of her puzzle. God was the worker putting the pieces together. Now she could look back and see the role that each had played in her life and their connections to Joel.

It was a quarter till five. A knock sounded on her apartment door. She hurried and opened it. Jack stood there nicely dressed in slacks, dinner jacket, and a necktie with a turkey on it. Naomi grinned. You never knew what to expect from him. He was fun. It was November and Thanksgiving wasn't far off.

"Are you my turkey this evening?" She laughed taking one finger and touching the bird on his tie. Then she straightened his tie which was a little crooked on purpose. Jack knew she would straighten it. It was part of who she was. "I have wrung the necks of a few turkeys in my time and then baked them."

"It is better to have my neck wrung by you, than some English woman who doesn't know what she is doing. I can see myself being wrung and roasted by you."

"I just don't know what you are going to do without me the next two months. Your ties need me. Does Karen know how many neckties I have straightened before sending you on dates with her?"

"When you have a beer or two in you, your date's necktie isn't a priority. I just might buy her a ring if she wasn't such a damn drunk." He stated lying to see her face. He had no intentions of ever buying Karen a ring. He was just putting in his time waiting for Naomi to discover that it was him that really loved her. Also, he used the word damn once in a while just to hear her scold him.

"You are awful. Karen is not drinking as much, since she has been dating you." Naomi replied. Then she took her fingers and pinched his cheek lightly and said. "I am going to wash your mouth out with soap if I hear you use that inappropriate word, damn, in my presence again. Little boys never learn. You would not be in trouble with me, if you would use the word only in the out-house where it belongs. It is a potty mouth word."

Jack grinned at her. Her fingers pinching his cheek, was sending unbelievable currents of electricity thru him. He reached up and pulled her fingers down and kissed them. "I will attempt to refrain from using my potty mouth word in your presence. You are the best mom a big boy could ever have.

Naomi smiled. "It is going to take me another three years or so to train you. You are a slow learner. How many times have I showed you how to straighten your tie?"

He released her hand. He knew what the limits were when it came to touching her. One day, she would be his. He just had to be patient.

"It takes a special mom with a lot of patience to train a big, slow, boy like me. Don't give up on me."

"You are the best friend that I have. I will never give up on you. I might wash your mouth out with soap, but I will never give up on you or not love you. I appreciate all that you have done for me, including my new shoes, gold safety pin, and material for two new dresses. You seem to sense what I need. Thank You. All my money has gone to my divorce attorney. Have I told you that Mr. Maynard thinks my divorce court date will be the first week in January? I am looking forward to being free from my nightmare."

"When that date comes, I am taking you out and buying you the biggest steak ever to celebrate. Marcus will just have to move over for one night."

"You have asked me first, I will celebrate with you first. Marcus will indeed have to wait his turn."

"Are you ready? I have reservations for us down at the Bistro." He stated as she checked her pinned pocket. She always carried her mad money, as she called it, in her dress pocket secured by a safety pin.

"Yes, I am ready. I must be back here at six. Marcus and I are to have a long talk tonight. A walk down by the river will be a first for us. I don't dare tell him that you and I have been down there many times walking on Sunday evenings. You I have trusted. Myself with him, I have not."

"I will have you back here on time, Sweet Thing. You can always depend on me. Just don't sit on our bench with him."

Naomi reached up and put her hand gently on his cheek. "I will never tell him about our bench. What is ours is ours." She stated. Then removing her hand she added. "You look very nice tonight. Karen is going to be pleased when you show up at her door later in the evening."

Jack didn't reply to the Karen reference. She had called and left a message on his answering earlier in the day stating that she never wanted to see him again, but not saying why. He really didn't care. In a little over two months, Naomi would be free and he had every intention dating and marrying Naomi. Karen was just a false face that he had worn till now. Naomi was his Sweet Thing.

The Bistro downtown was an upscale restaurant. They would not serve you unless you were wearing a jacket if you were a man and a dress if you were a woman; not even if you were there just for carry out. Jack always took Naomi there when he was celebrating the closing of some case. Naomi was sure that tonight was for that reason also. Normally, he showed up at her door to chat a few minutes on Saturday nights in jeans and collared sport shirts before taking Karen out. He always told her that Karen was not a bistro girl. They usually did fast food and the movies. Naomi always inspected him to make sure he didn't have a hair out of place, before he went down to Karen's apartment. It had become a ritual. He came home to Naomi before going out with Karen. Naomi never asked what Jack and Karen did after the movies. She did not want to know. For one thing, she still remembered how wonderful making love to Jack was in her dream. She did not want to spoil that fantasy by picturing him in bed with someone else. She did not know why, but she was a little bit jealous of Karen when it came to Jack.

"I am in the mood for one of the Bistro's mushroom steak burgers with some of that French onion dipping sauce. You know, I will have to send my dinner jacket to the cleaners afterward."

"One day, I will get you trained so that you don't make such a mess with your dripping burgers. I just don't know what you did before me. Did you have another Naomi before me to wipe your mouth, straighten your tie, and see that you were presentable?"

"You are the only Sweet Thing that has ever cared enough to straighten my tie. I have been too busy getting my detective business going to chase sweet dishes like you. One day, I just might take the time to chase you. Should I do that, I will be in one heck of a mess."

"Why would you be in a mess?"

""If I caught you, Karen would kill me and you." He replied grinning. Jack always let her believe his thoughts and heart belonged to Karen. As long as he did, she would go to dinner or anywhere else with him.

"I am told that red heads are mean. It is best that you not rile her. I would hate to have my special friend die at the hands of an angry woman. Plus, I would miss wiping your face and straightening your tie. However, I think I could hold my own with Karen and possibly even protect you. You could hide behind my skirt tail like my son Adam did when he was little. He was afraid of mean red dogs."

"You see why I need you? I am in love with a red haired dog of a woman with a long red tail who is capable of killing me."

"Little boys always run home to their mama's. You are no different. Hide behind my skirt tail if you need to." She snickered. "Should the red haired dog ever try to bite or kill you, I will look at her and say, 'Bad dog . . . go away and leave my Jackie alone.'"

"I will always run home to you Naomi." He stated.

She then picked up her door key and her attorney's prepaid cell phone off of her kitchen table.

"Come on Sweet Thing, it is burger time." He replied opening her front door for her.

"I am really hungry. The market got busy during lunch time and I did not get a chance to eat. I hope you can afford me. I have a healthy appetite this evening."

He laughed and then they continued their conversation as they descended the stairs from the third floor.

"Dan Maynard told me about your divorce court date being moved up. I am really happy for you Naomi. In case you are wondering, the new court date is what we are celebrating this evening."

At the bottom of the stairs, they stopped for a breather and Naomi turned to face Jack. "Only you know how pleased I am to have my nightmare coming to an end. I also know now where you have been on all of the Saturdays that you were missing from the market. Dan told me today that you are his detective and you took on my case free of charge. You have kept secrets from me." She laughed kissing him on the cheek. "I am a real dummy."

"It was best you didn't know that I was working on your case. Besides, I wanted you to like me for me, not for my snooping nose." He stated as they stepped over to the street curb and he helped her into the passenger side of his plain, gray sedan.

"I rather like your snoopy nose and your four eyes please me to." She replied as he got in the driver's side and buckled up. Jack wore eyeglasses.

"Just so you know, Karen cancelled our date tonight. She didn't give me a reason."

"You do not seem to be unhappy about it. Why?" She asked as he turned on the radio to some gospel music for her. He had introduced her to it and she was becoming quite a fan of the different quartets.

"I have the other prettiest woman in Paducah on my arm. I am one lucky man with no reason to be unhappy."

"Karen is far prettier than me, but thank you for saying so."

"I don't know what is up with Karen, but she might be seeing someone besides me. There is also the possibility that she has heard from her ex. She is a sucker for him and he may be trying to con her again. I want you to be careful and peep out your door before opening it this week." He stated as they turned down into the business district.

"Do you know how much I appreciate your friendship, Jack?" Naomi asked.

"Yes, Sweet Thing, I know." He replied. "I also know that you plan to walk away after next week leaving Paducah behind. I hope that does not include me. I travel all over in my line of business. There is no reason I can't drive or fly to wherever you end up. There is no reason for you to walk away from me."

"You know me better than I possibly know myself." She replied. "Marcus and Karen have become dear friends to me. However, they are connected to my Joel. I cannot stay here once they find out who I am. My friendships and world here will cease to be. The scandal will be big. I am sure that you will be my only friend left standing. I will not be able to return to the market and hold my head up in the spring because of it."

"I do know you better that you know yourself, Sweet Thing. To love someone, you care enough to get to know them inside and out. You are the only family I have, Naomi. My parents are gone and I am an only child. This detective has been too busy chasing bad guys to get married or have children. You are my Sunday dinner girl. When I am with you, I am home. I will come home to you, no matter where you go."

"That is how I feel about you. I am an orphan and my two children are dead. When the chips fall next week, I am sure that it will be only you left standing with me, just as you were the one supporting me the evening Jenkins slapped me. I was wrong calling Marcus a dog!"

"If you truly love someone, Naomi, you will be there for them in the good and the bad. Perhaps you went a little crazy in the tongue department! However, you were then and still are my Sunday dinner girl and I will never let you down."

"Have I thanked you properly for my new shoes and the material you left on my table for new dresses? I will make myself the new dresses tomorrow. The new shoes, I have on, will be my traveling on into a new life shoes."

"As long as those shoes keep bringing you back to me, I am okay with that. I have been thinking about buying myself a new pair of traveling shoes. Which direction are your shoes going to take you?"

"I haven't decided yet. I know I cannot stay here once the news of Joel hits the papers. I do not wish to be known as the wife of a polygamist. I wish to be known for who I am and who I have become. How would you feel, if I told you that I was thinking of becoming a holiness lady minister?"

"Well, Sweetie, you are my Sunday dinner girl and if that includes a little pew sitting for me, so be it."

"Your words please me, Jack. I was not sure if you would still want to be my friend should I speak and take a serious stand against sin and the devil. I intend to preach Hell hot and holiness of dress and actions."

"I need my sinful ass scorched a little. I would rather it be you do the scorching than the devil someday." He replied laughing.

Jack parked his car across from the Bistro and in front of the building he owned where he had a loft apartment upstairs with a balcony overlooking the street.

"Would you mind if we spend a few minutes upstairs on my balcony before walking over to the Bistro? I forgot my cell phone and I can't afford to miss any important calls with us winding down into your last week. I am still following a few leads."

"That will be nice. I love looking at the river from up there and down into the windows of the shops below lining the street. The view from your balcony is exciting. I know that I am not to embrace graven images, but I would love to have a photo of you with the river behind you, to look at, when I am lonesome for you. I will be hiding out for two months after I go visit a friend and attend a wedding next weekend with her."

"That can be taken care of." He laughed. "I will get my camera and you can snap a photo of me standing on the balcony and then me you. We will both have a graven image photo to look at when we are lonesome for each other."

Jack had never dared to photograph her before. She was Amish and she avoided all cameras. He tried to never do anything that would rock his boat with her.

After climbing the outside flight of stairs on the side of Jack's building, above his detective agency, Naomi remained on the balcony while Jack entered his apartment to retrieve his cell phone and camera. When he returned, he snapped a picture of her with the river behind her in the distance and then she did the same after he showed her how to work the camera. Afterward, he showed her the photos on the digital screen on the back of his camera. She squealed with delight. Then they turned and stood side by side at the balcony railing looking out over the town, the river, and the main street below which ran between them and the Bistro. She had her hand resting on the balcony railing. Jack placed his hand on top of hers. She let him because she felt safe in his presence.

"No matter where you go, Naomi, make your way back to me. We are family and my arms will always be open to you no matter what. I have put your name on my checking and savings. I don't want you out there somewhere doing without shoes and things you need. What is mine is yours, no questions asked. Make your way back to me or let me come to you. I know that you are in love with Marcus. That may change in the next few months. If it does, my arms are always yours and waiting?"

"Thank you, Jack! I trust you and your arms."

CHAPTER ELEVEN

Marcus and Karen Kiss

At about a quarter after five, Marcus parked his jeep in public parking down by the river. He headed for the Bistro sticking his arms in his dinner jacket as he went. The bistro was upscale and you didn't get in the door without a jacket, even if it was just for carry out. He wasn't overly thrilled with Angela's demand for food from there. It was expensive and he was saving his money for an engagement ring for Naomi. He had no savings, thanks to his sister. Angela had depleted all of his savings over the years. He couldn't count the number of times he had paid attorney and bail bondsmen fees to keep her out of jail for writing hot checks, etc. Angela was his money pit.

About half way to the Bistro, Karen stumbled out of the doorway of a drinking establishment and stumbled into him almost falling. He lost his balance, but quickly regained his stance and then steadied her.

"Damn you Karen, why are you tying one on so early in the evening?" He asked putting his arm around her waist to steady her. "You should know better than to get sloppy drunk wearing four inch spikes. You are asking to have a serious fall and break a leg."

"I can't get a d . . . divorce." She replied slurring her words and giggling. "I am not married."

"I gather you must have seen your divorce attorney today, and the meeting was not a good one." He replied holding on to her. She was limp like a rag doll in his arms."

"I have been conned by Jack and N. . . Naomi." She sputtered leaning heavy into him.

"Well, walk down to the Bistro with me. I will buy you a cup of coffee and you can tell me what your attorney said while I wait on my take out order. I have company coming in from out of town and I am feeding them the easy way with carry out."

"Why aren't you with your pre . . . precious Naomi?" She smirked in a slurred voice. "It is Saturday night."

"I am picking my sister and kids up at the bus station in a few minutes. I must get them settled in at my place before I can pick up Naomi. Naomi is having a quick burger with your Jack and then we have a scheduled walk down by the river at six. Don't you have a date with Jack, later?" He asked as she took one hand and patted his backside.

"Nope . . . he . . . he is history." She stated getting in Marcus' face.

"You have serious alcohol breath, Karen." He stated as he removed her hand from the rear of his trousers.

"I should have dated you, not Jack." She replied taking one hand and patting his backside again. "I should have chosen pro . . . professor long legs." Then she drunkenly giggled.

"So, you are drunk because you and Jack have had a spat of some sort?" He asked holding tightly to her. Her four inch spikes were wobbling and not moving in a pretty fashion. He ignored her roaming hands. She was drunk as a skunk and had rubber in her knees.

"Jack is a damn detective hired by Naomi to take my apartment complex from me." She sputtered.

"You are drunk, Karen. Whatever your attorney said to you today is getting mixed up in your head with your thoughts about Jack and Naomi. It is your husband Joey that wants to get his hands on your apartment complex."

"I am indeed d . . . drunk." She stated. "You should be. Naomi . . . Naomi is Jack's birthday girl. I got a book for my birthday yes . . . yesterday. He gave her a two thousand dollar, gold, designer safe . . . safety pin. It is my birthday and I . . . I got a damn book from him. I was hope . . . hoping for a ring."

"He paid what for the gold safety pin that Naomi is securing her pocket with?" Marcus asked suddenly alarmed.

"He pa . . . paid two thou . . . thousand dollars, plus tax. I saw the receipt on his kitchen table. I forgot he was out . . . out of town on a case. A jewelry catalog lay open on his table along with the receipt." She muttered and then suddenly threw both of her arms around his neck. "Take me, I am now yours."

"You are going to hate yourself tomorrow, Karen, when you remember this. God forbid you had stumbled out into the street and into the arms of a stranger. He might have taken you, your purse, your virginity or lack of it, and whatever else he could get from you. This is the river district."

"Jack is in love with your N . . . Naomi. I always won. . . wondered why he wouldn't sleep with me." She blurted out in a slur. "He has been date . . . dating me to be near her. What does she have that I don't have, other than plain Jane, cheap ass, ugly, black, old lady's shoes? I have spikes and pre . . . pretty legs."

"Yes, you do have pretty legs, but currently they are not so pretty. They are sticks of wobbling rubber." He stated stopping and steadying her once more.

Then out of nowhere, she threw both arms around his neck and kissed him. He didn't have a free arm to prevent it. He had both arms around her waist at that point, holding her up.

"How was . . . was that?" She asked laying her head over on his shoulder. "I can kiss and satisfy a man. I just don't know why my Joey mar . . . married Naomi or why my J . . . Jack bought her jewelry. She is too tight laced to kiss either of them like that."

"You are drunk and have your friends and your divorce all mixed up in your head." Marcus stated thinking she was rambling drunkenly out of her gourd.

"Jack's pin is the same thing as an en . . . engagement in ring in his eyes. Naomi does not wear jewelry, He has p . . . pinned her. You and I are suckers. Naomi and Jack must b . . . be lovers."

"You are not making sense, Karen. I know for a fact that Naomi loves me. She told me so today. We have a date at six. For the first time she has agreed to walk down by the river with me. You are drunk and messing up your facts. I am sorry Jack got you a book for your birthday. We all have had our relationship problems and disappointments. Take yours up with Jack, not a bottle of vodka. God . . . your breath is bad."

On the second floor balcony of the building across from the bistro, Jack and Naomi stood looking down at the street. Suddenly, Jack got a funny expression on his face. He removed his hand from the top of Naomi's and grabbed his digital camera from his pants pocket. That was a natural response for him. He was a private detective.

"Aren't you to meet Marcus in less than an hour?" Jack asked with a shocked look on his face.

"He told me he might be five or ten minutes late because he has an after-hours plumber coming to work on a sink problem in his house. Why?"

"Well, Naomi. You and I have been had." He said pointing to the street below and the sidewalk across the street. A couple was walking with their arms around each other and the woman had her hand on the man's backside. "She doesn't look like any kitchen sink plumber I have ever had."

Naomi looked down and across the street and then gasped taking a death grip on the balcony rail in front of her. She bit her lip to hold back tears. Jack seeing her tense up stated. "It is okay, Sweet Thing. I have your backside and he raised the camera to take photos of his Karen in the arms of Marcus walking toward the bistro."

"I have been a fool. Marcus was playing a game with me today when he told me he loved me. Let me take these photos, Jack." Naomi stated releasing her death grip on the rail. "He will not be able to deny the photos, if I take them. Karen must be the married lover he refers to."

Meanwhile, down on the street, Marcus stopped walking with Karen for a moment or so to get a new grip on her waist to steady her. She had a bad case of roaming hands, but he ignored them knowing she needed his help to get her home safely. Getting a new grip on her, he once more started walking toward the bistro with her and her roaming hands. However, suddenly, it was not his backside that she was going for. Embarrassed at her having her hand patting his trouser's fly, he stopped walking again and took her roaming fly hand and placed it around his neck. Then he returned both of his arms to her waist to steady her once more. Then they resumed walking towards the bistro. He decided he would pour coffee down her till his carry out order was ready. Then, he would drive her home before picking up Angela and the kids at the bus station.

He glanced at his watch. There was no way he was going to make it to Naomi's apartment by six or six fifteen. He would have to tell Naomi that the plumber took a little longer than he had planned. He was sure it would be six-thirty or possibly seven by the time he disposed of Karen and then picked up Angela and her kids. He had waited for over a year for Naomi to be willing to step outside the farmer's market or Karen's apartment with him. Angela and Karen were messing up the most important evening of his life and there wasn't a damn thing he could do about it.

In the invisible, Frankie Frances and Osceola stood on the balcony with Naomi who was snapping shots of Marcus in a compromising position with Karen's hands all over him in front of the bistro.

"He is in the dog house again, isn't he Ms. Osceola black Lightning?" Frankie Frances asked eyeing Marcus below and a big red dog, standing on its two back feet, running its front paw down the front of his trousers.

"The dog house does seem to be his preference for a home." Osceola replied in her syrupy, sticky, fly swatting voice.

"What does he see in her?" Frankie Frances asked with her glasses slid down on the end of her pimple covered teen nose. "That female dog has one of the worst, mangy, red tails I have ever seen. She will cost him a fortune in flea and tick dip."

"Push your glasses up where they belong, Frankie Frances. She is not a dog."

Frankie Frances pushed her glasses up her nose. "Oh . . . It is Karen in Marcus' arms."

"It is trouble in his arms." Osceola retorted pointing to Naomi who had a camera and was taking photos. "With every snap of that camera, her love for him is dying. There will be no walk down by the river for them tonight."

"Just give me your nail file sword, Ms. Osceola black Lightning. I will fly down there, turn Karen into a slithering snake and cut off Marcus' arms so he will never hug anyone but Naomi ever again." Frankie Frances replied in her honey dipped, young southern voice that had a hint of anger in it.

"We are not angels of vengeance, Frankie Frances. We are guardians. I let Jack forget his cell phone so Naomi could end up here and possibly discover that it is Jack that truly loves her. Marcus and Karen having an affair is a surprise even to me." Osceola retorted. "He is not our concern, nor is Karen."

"Karen is my concern." A voice stated. Osceola turned to see Corky Cameron standing in his military dress uniform grinning at her. "It has been a few years." He stated walking over and hugging her. "How has my death angel been?"

(Corky Cameron was a cousin of Karen, although he was no longer alive. Osceola Black Lightning had been his death angel six or so years prior and had transported him over to the other side. He was killed in a highway accident as he was on his way back to the military base, Ft. Wood in Missouri. He and a van of others had all died. Osceola transported his soul over as well as the two souls of Naomi's children. The three died the same week.

"I am fine, now that I have gotten a look at you. I don't recall you looking this handsome the night I pulled your soul from your wreck. You have a new body and it doesn't have severed parts or is covered in blood."

"I kind of like my new look myself." He replied looking down at his crisp, neatly pressed military uniform.

"So why are you here on the balcony with us in Paducah? God has an angel shortage and I am doing a short fill in stint as a guardian for the white cap named Naomi standing there taking photos." Osceola added.

"Karen down there is my cousin. She agreed to watch my dog till I got out of the army. She is still keeping my dog, even though I am dead. I owe her. When God asked me what position I felt I would be the happiest performing in Heaven, I suggested that he make me a spirit guide. So, here I am."

"May I ask what you are doing standing up here speaking with us when your drunk assignment is down there?" Osceola asked pointing to Karen down on the sidewalk in front of the bistro in Marcus' arms.

"I saw Naomi standing up here. We are old friends, in case you have forgotten." Corky stated as Jack entered his apartment to answer an inside phone line that was ringing.

Naomi lowered her camera and turned around with tears in her eyes. Instantly, her eyes lit up seeing a familiar face. "Corky . . . how is my friend? Have you found that special girl with sloppy kisses?"

Corky took Naomi's hand. "I am still looking for a girl with a wagging tail!" He replied referring to a conversation they had the year before when they had first arrived at Karen's apartment complex after riding a bus together.

Osceola rolled her eyes and muttered in the invisible as Naomi and Corky chatted along the railing. "I wish he was looking for a girl with a wagging tongue. Frankie Frances Periwinkle would be all his."

"I heard that, Ms. Osceola Black Lightning." Frankie Frances sputtered who proceeded to take one of her dog leashes and twirled it lassoing a flower pot hanging above Osceola's head. Instantly, the pot that had just been watered earlier was tipped and all the wet soil showered Osceola in the invisible. The pot then set itself back up straight.

"Take this!" Osceola replied mad in her syrupy, sticky, fly swatting voice.

Osceola swished her nail file at a vine of Honeysuckle that was growing up the side of the building. Instantly, the blooms shot off of it and covered Frankie Frances scrubbing her skin like they were tiny wash cloths. Then the returned to their spots on the vine they had broken off of. Frankie Frances began to sniff and tears welled up in her eyes.

"You have smeared me with the smell of Honeysuckle. That scent is for little girls, Ms. Osceola Black Lightning. I will never catch a guy smelling like a seven year old girl."

"Well, if he were here, do you think my long legged Jack Rabbit would be happy to see me with wet soil on my hair, in my mouth, and down between my endowments?"

"You played unfair. The Honeysuckle will not wash off for days and there is a good looking guy standing on this porch. He will think I am a baby."

Frankie Frances began to wail and instantly it started raining all around the balcony where they stood as well onto the sidewalk in front of the bistro. Marcus quickly helped Karen inside.

"Okay . . . okay. Enough is enough." Osceola stated with her fingers in her ears. "I will get rid of the Honeysuckle smell. In a flash, she grabbed Frankie Frances by her pony tail, swung her over the railing, and held her dangling by her ponytail while the rain showered her, clothes and all. Then she pulled her back on to the balcony in a soaked to the skin and spitting water state with Corky Cameron standing leaning on the railing grinning at her in her wet school girl clothes. Naomi had stepped inside the apartment to give Jack his camera.

"What are you looking at?" Frankie Frances screeched while taking her water laden glasses from the end of her nose and drying them on a dry porch chair cushion. "Haven't you ever seen a wet T-shirt girl before?"

Corky Cameron bit his lip and turned away trying not to burst into laughter. She was humorous and cute for a little kid. Also, she had nothing to enter a wet T-shirt contest with. Then he saw Marcus disappearing into the bistro with Karen so he snapped his fingers and he disappeared.

"Back to business, Frankie Frances, we are supposed to be guarding Naomi. Do you want Corky to think you are a misfit angel who can do nothing but walk dogs?"

Frankie Frances bit her lip and gave Osceola the evil eye. Osceola grinned knowing she had got her. Then she swished her nail file sword a little and all the dirty mess removed itself from her and the evening in Parish blue-purple stilettos and matching cocktail dress studded with diamonds she was wearing.

Frankie Frances turned back to smile and flirt with Corky, but he was gone. Disappointed, she turned back to Osceola to take care of business.

"We should do something, Ms. Osceola Black Lightning! Marcus is breaking Naomi's heart. Shouldn't we protect her heart somehow?" Frankie Frances asked in her honey dipped, young, southern voice.

"In order for her to move on to her future, Marcus has to do what he is the best at, screwing up. If all went well here for him and her, she would not move past him and become who she is to be one day. A broken heart is but a stepping stone to the next phase of her life." Osceola replied in her syrupy voice while pulling out her nail file to work on her nails which were already perfectly manicured.

Suddenly, Corky Cameron popped back on to the balcony in the invisible. Naomi was still inside of Jack's apartment.

Corky pulled a sword from a side sheath, rested its tip on the floor, and then leaned on it like it was a walking cane.

"Why don't you move on and past your long legged Jack Rabbit, Ms. Osceola Black Lightning? You are living in the past. You should be stepping forward to meet the mate god has prepared for you and waits for you somewhere outside the Eastern Gate. Why are you hanging on to your broken heart and the past?"

"Why are you hanging onto eye glasses that should have been replaced years ago?" Osceola replied in a huff. "When you replace those glasses, then I will talk to you about replacing my Jack rabbit. Till then, the subject of my broken heart and love for my long legged Jack Rabbit is off limits to you."

Corky grinned looking at the very young angel who was letting Osceola have it with her mouth. No angel in Heaven ever dared to lock horns with the death angel standing beside him, known as Black Lightning. She had a reputation for bending halos out of shape and making God squirm.

"Tut – tut, Ms. Osceola black Lightning. You are being a little testy with me. I am sorry that you can't take it when I tell you the truth about yourself. You should listen to me and throw your broken heart away. I would never be so stupid as to hold on to one. That is the difference between you and me. I know when to move on."

"You haven't even had your first boyfriend yet, Frankie Frances. Give me advice when you have had some experience under your belt. Of course in my thinking right now, you are never going to have a boyfriend to have an experience with. Your mouth makes you ugly." Osceola huffed.

Corky Cameron wanted to go to the rescue of the young angel, but he didn't dare cross Osceola by wading into her mouth war with the girl. He knew better. With one swish of her nail file, she could transport him back to Heaven and dump him in God's trash can. He was no match for her. She was God's number one death angel and a force that no one messed with.

"I am going to tell God on you, Ms. Osceola black Lightning. It is not nice to tell someone they are ugly. God doesn't make ugly, guardian angels." Frankie Frances replied in her honey dipped, southern voice with tears filling her eyes. "Only death angels are ugly. They have to be, to scare the life out of humans. You are the ugly one and you are taking it out on me."

A booming voice echoed in the invisible sky above Osceola, Frankie, and Corky Cameron.

"Don't antagonize the dog walker. I am tired of hearing her dog crap complaints."

Osceola grinned and yelled back. "Better your ears filled with doggie doo, than mine." Then she grabbed Frankie Frances' arm and pulled her as far back under the balcony awning as she could, leaving an oblivious Corky to suffer the consequences . Sure enough, it rained doggie- do in the invisible and corky Cameron was one brown mess. He spit and sputtered and looked at his dress uniform in disbelief.

"I think you are on God's list again, Ms. Osceola black Lightning." Frankie Frances stated in her know it all voice.

"The crap didn't land on me, did it?" Osceola asked in her syrupy, sticky, southern voice while pointing at Corky. "He must be on God's list."

"He is definitely one dirty dog!" Frankie Frances stated with her eye glasses perched crooked on the end of her nose. "May I keep him, if I clean him up and promise to feed and water him? I have a leash in my back pack."

Osceola reached over with her finger extended and pushed Frankie Frances' eye glasses up her nose and into place. "Now what do you see?"

"A long legged Jack Rabbit man named Corky." Frankie Frances replied sighing. "How old is he?"

"Quit drooling, Frankie Frances. You are thirteen going on fourteen and he is eighteen. He is too old for you. He likes girls with cleavage and clear faces. You are a little lacking in both of those departments."

Tears rolled down Frankie Frances's face. "Just because I am a thirty triple A and you are a forty-four triple E, doesn't mean that I am not a gorgeous woman. Your reference to the pimples on my face was unnecessary. I am adding the comment to my list to tell God about when I get home. I hope he deflates your boob job and gives you a case of leprosy for your remark about my face. I am going to ask him to."

"Be my guest when we get home! I am sure that God is going to be one happy man seeing you coming."

When Osceola was distracted by Marcus exiting the bistro alone, Corky leaned down and whispered in Frankie Frances's ear. "I don't go for obese, big boobs and I have an occasional need for pimple crème myself. Soda and chocolate make me break out."

Frankie Frances grinned at him and her tears went away. He didn't know it yet, but he was going to be her long legged Jack Rabbit man. Now, she just had to convince Osceola, to let her date him. Maybe she would just elope with him, if he ever asked.

Corky Cameron then ignored Frankie Frances, snapped his fingers, and was once more gone to see why Karen was not on Marcus' arm.

Jack and Naomi stepped out of his apartment and proceeded to lock the apartment door. Walking to the railing, they saw that Marcus and Karen were no longer on the curb below, so they descended the side stairs. Reaching the bottom, Jack took Naomi's hand and held it for a moment or so searching for words.

"I had no idea Marcus and Karen would be down there when I brought you up here to retrieve my cell phone. I am really sorry, Naomi. I wouldn't purposely hurt you or make you cry for any reason."

"He is what he is, a user of married women. This one has surprised me." She replied.

"I may be a detective, but I definitely did not see this one coming. My red head and Marcus fondling each other is unbelievable. I would not have believed it, hadn't I seen it with my own eyes." Jack stated with a shocked voice. "He has always told me how crazy he is about you."

"I have been a fool, Jack. Would you consider letting me stay with you for the next week till I leave for Missouri to go to a wedding. Mr. Maynard's phone has not wrung yet, but it is time for me to move out of my apartment now that I have seen them together."

"Sweet Thing, you don't have to ask. Whatever is mine is yours and that includes my apartment. I will sleep on the couch. You can have my bed. I don't want my Sunday dinner girl not getting her beauty rest."

Naomi smiled and then remembered the dream she had months before. Jack had said the same thing to her in her dream. Looking into his eyes, she suddenly saw a man that loved her, really loved her. Was that what the dream was all about? Was God trying to show her in the dream who was to be in her future?"

"Are you sad over losing Karen?" Naomi asked.

"I am not sad, just shocked. My friend Marcus pulled a fast one on me."

"Well . . ." Naomi replied, cringing at how close she had come to walking by the river with Marcus and making an idiot out of herself telling him that she loved him. "Now, I know who his plumber is."

"Come on Sweet Thing. We are not going to let them ruin our evening. Instead of a bistro burger, I have suddenly decided you and I want T-bones from the steak house. I think my Sunday girl might also be in need of a big piece of chocolate pie. I might just eat one myself."

"You are right about the chocolate pie! Without it, I might do something to my landlord that I would regret."

"For you, two pieces of chocolate pie are on our agenda." Jack stated laughing. "Just so you know, Naomi. I have never slept with her."

"I am sorry that I have made such a fool out of myself over Marcus. You have always been the one that has stood by me. You should turn me over your knee and spank me. I am always threatening to discipline you."

"Maybe I like you threatening to discipline me." He stated winking at her and then grinning. "Come on! Let us get our first evening started. We don't have to be in any hurry because your date at six doesn't look like it is happening. It is a quarter till now."

"I did tell him to be on time." She replied trying not to cry.

Jack put his arm around her. "Go ahead and cry if you need to. I will love you just the same."

Naomi turned to Jack, then, she threw her arms around him and buried her face in his chest and cried. He put his arms around her and held her close, resting his chin on the top of her little white cap. When she sniffled and dried her eyes, he offered her his arm.

"Do you want to go sit in front of your apartment till six, just so you will never have any doubts?" Jack asked as he helped her in the passenger side of his gray sedan.

"Yes, I wish to sit till six-thirty. I never want him to say that it was I that stood him up. I told him to be there at six."

"At six thirty, we head for the steak house and chocolate pie." He stated helping her into his car.

Jack had stayed six weeks with Naomi the previous winter after having surgery. She had rescued him from the hospital when he had no one to go home to. Although they had just been vendor friends, she had walked to the hospital everyday in the snow to visit him and then nursed him for six weeks afterward. He hadn't forgotten all the bed pans and urinals she had emptied for him when he had only known her for a few months. It didn't matter whether Naomi loved him. She was number one with him and always would be. Falling in love with her had been easy. Watching her get hurt by Marcus was not so.

Marcus had been Jack's best friend all thru high school, college, and afterward. They were both farm boy transplants who now enjoyed the market as a way of keeping their Missouri childhood farm memories alive. Jack had gone thru college on money he had received from an insurance settlement. His parents had died in a car wreck. Marcus made his way thru college selling him-self to rich, older women for tuition and book money. Jenkins had paid for his master's degree as well as coughed up the down payment on the house he now was making payments on. Now they were both educated men, friends with good jobs, and both in love with the same woman.

In Jack's mind, Naomi was too good for Marcus. After meeting Naomi, he saw his friend for the first time for what he really was, a gigolo. He was just a higher class form of Angela, his prostitute sister. Before Naomi, Jack had just seen the two of them as confirmed bachelors playing the field. Since Naomi, Jack had abandoned all of his dating except for Karen. He knew that Naomi was everything he wanted in a woman and he was willing to live a life in the holiness church or any other life style that Naomi chose.

In the invisible, Frankie Frances day dreamed about Corky Cameron. He was the handsomest man she had ever seen, even if his military uniform had been soiled with doggie-doo. It took a woman's touch to keep a man looking nice and she was sure that she was that woman.

CHAPTER TWELVE

The Adoption

After leaving Karen in the care of a friend of hers who happened to be inside the bistro, Marcus sprinted to his jeep carrying his plastic bag of carry out knowing how late he was. However, he had told Naomi that he might be a little late due to a plumbing problem. He glanced at his watch. It was five minutes till six. He knew Angela's demand for bistro food had put a serious kink in his evening. Next, he ran thru Dee's fast food picking up some kid's meals for Adam and Mary. The baby wasn't big enough for anything but milk, yet. He had that in his refrigerator. Then he sped for the bus stop.

Arriving at the bus station, he spotted Angela and three very visibly, dirty kids sitting and waiting on him. He was not happy at what he saw. His sister always brought her kids dirty and hungry. He needed to get to Naomi, not feed and clean up three dirty kids. It was a big night for him and he was longing to hear Naomi say once more that she loved him. He had waited a year and a half for those words to spill from her mouth.

After loading the two older kids in the back of his jeep and making them sit on the floor, he helped Angela and the baby in. She hadn't brought car seats or anything for them.

"The bus driver let you on the bus with no car seats for Mary and Martha?" He asked not believing how thoughtless his sister was.

"Where do you think I would come up with money for bus tickets? I hitch hiked." She replied closing the door of the jeep. "My last ride let me off here so it would be convenient for you to pick me up."

"You are unbelievable, Angela. A stranger could have taken advantage of you or the kids."

"I paid him for the ride!" She stated as the baby began to waken and whine, which she ignored.

"Just how much cash did you give him? You just told me you didn't have money for bus tickets."

"There are other ways of paying a man without forking over cash." She replied as though prostitution was a socially acceptable topic like any other.

"Don't talk like that in front of your kids."

"Get a life, Marcus. Mary and Martha will grow up and be whores, just like me. I want my mother to be ashamed of them, just like she is me. That way, her grandchildren will never have anything to do with her, just like I don't."

"Mom may be strict and set in her ways, Angela, but your kids are missing out on a lot of farm life experiences that could be good for them. Everyday existence in low income housing isn't exactly a great introduction to life." He replied as he pulled into his drive way. He then helped every one out. Mary and Adam made a mad dash for the kitchen and straight to the refrigerator once he opened the door.

After pulling Adam and Mary away from a leftover container of cold fries and half a three day old burger, he set them at his kitchen table and gave them their kid's meals. There wasn't a doubt in his mind that they hadn't been fed all day. He turned to converse with Angela. She was standing at the kitchen counter eating her expensive bistro meal straight from its foam tray with her fingers.

"For God's sake, Angela, I have forks." He replied pulling a drawer open and handing her one.

"Lighten up, Marcus. I will eat with my fingers if I want. Save the etiquette for your rich, married lovers."

"I am late for my date, Angela. Tell me quickly what it is that you have insisted on ruining my evening for. Then you and the kids can crash and I will be back later tonight."

"What is one lady friend to you? Women flaunt themselves at you, they always have. You are not wanting for a piece of tail." She replied ignoring the baby who was whining laying on the kitchen floor.

"You should really tone down your language in front of your kids. Don't you want them to grow up and fit in with a better crowd than you run with? Adam's mouth has become so foul that I don't dare take him to the market with me, for fear he will say something inappropriate to the women vendors there. You really need to think about how you are raising them and what you are saying in front of them."

"Forget his foul mouth, Marcus. Once Joe marries me, I am dumping him and his sisters into foster care. Let someone else worry about their foul mouths and manners. They are just free housing, food stamps, and a welfare check to me."

"Surely you do not mean that?" He questioned shaking his head.

Angela ignored his reply and continued. "Joe's tattoo business, in St. Louis, is now turning big profits. He came home to me with a huge stash of bills in his wallet. He has finally hit the big time. I won't be needing welfare on this baby of his that I am carrying." She stated rubbing her belly and smiling. "I am going to keep this baby, it is his. The other three can take a hike."

Marcus shook his head in disgust. "Why in the hell did you ever have them, Angela? It isn't like you don't know what birth control is."

"Joe likes kids. I needed something to make him hold on to me. He thinks they are his. Every time I thought he was going to abandon me, I would get pregnant by one of my Johns and ask him not to leave till after the baby was born. Each time I told him that I thought I was carrying twins. He has a fascination with twins. Anyway, it worked. He has wandered some over the years, but he always comes back. He seems to be fond of Adam, who actually might be his, I am not sure. I slept with a lot of men the week he was conceived."

"You have your priorities all wrong, Angela. You should have children because you want them and your partner wants them. You don't have babies to hold on to someone and then neglect them. Mom never neglected us. We were fed, clean, and had regular mealtimes and bedtimes. She may have been strict, but she was a good mother. You could be a good mother if you tried."

"Motherhood is not for me. I have better things to do with my time. Adam, Mary, and Martha are just food stamps, welfare money, and free public housing. I went thru the pains of labor having them for Joe, they owe me."

Exasperated and appalled at his sister's self- centered indifference, he tried to speed up the conversation. His night with Naomi was where he wanted to be.

"Aren't you eating?" Angela asked sitting her half empty container down on the cabinet and checking out his refrigerator for something to drink. She pulled out his carton of milk and then closed the fridge door.

"I have a dinner date, remember?" He retorted as she drank the last of his milk straight from its container. She gave no thought to the fact that her baby was lying hungry on the floor.

"Well, cancel your date. I am leaving the kids with you for the next week. I need the time to get my act together." She replied, caring less whether he had plans. "I just have a week to plan my wedding and buy a dress. You wouldn't have five hundred that you could loan me, do you?"

"Damn you, Angela. I have a lady friend that I am serious about, and I am saving to buy her an engagement ring. No, I don't have five hundred. In case you have forgotten, I sent you a thousand last month so you could pay your bail bondsman." He stated checking the time on his watch.

"Be prepared, I am going to need another thousand next month to pay an attorney to get me out of that little scrape with the law. I was only shoplifting a couple of outfits for Adam and Mary to wear in my wedding. You are taking your niece and nephew for the next week! I told them they were going to get to stay with you for a few days. Do you want them to think they have an uncaring jerk for an uncle?"

"I can't exactly waltz over to my lady friend's house tonight with three dirty kids in tow." He replied mad and wondering how he was going to get a message to Naomi. Karen was drunk and Naomi didn't have a phone. He looked at his watch. It was a quarter till seven.

"If she likes you, like every woman you have ever met, she will be there a week from now." Angela replied flippantly.

"Last spring, you dumped your kids on me for a couple of days and it turned into five weeks. I have a life and want children of my own."

"Well, aren't you selfish?" She replied taunting him. "Next Saturday, I am dumping the three of them for good into the foster care system and you won't have to worry about them ever again. I am looking forward to starting over fresh with Joe and this baby of his that I am carrying. We may move to St. Louis. He likes it there for some reason. His many tattoo business related trips there, the last four or so years, has paid off."

"Damn you, Angela. You have got to understand, I can't take your kids right now. The woman I am dating is not fond of Adam. He said unbelievable, inappropriate things to her last spring. You are screwing up my chances for a life with her."

"Well, dump her and find some other rich bitch." She replied drinking the last of the milk as her baby started to sniffle and cry lying on the floor.

"What makes you think Joe is going to marry you, support the baby you are carrying, and love you forever. He has never given you a dime all the years he has wandered in and out of your life free loading off of you. When you give up these three kids, your food stamps, housing, and welfare money will cease. Do you really think Joe is going to step up to the plate and provide for you? He has taken advantage of you for nine or ten years. I don't recall anyone stepping up to the plate to help you, but me. Why would you even consider getting pregnant again? You are just going to ruin another child's life."

"Lighten up, Marcus. I know what I am doing. I brought you something." She stated ignoring what he had said. She started digging in her big sloppy handbag ignoring the baby that was now crying.

Marcus walked over to the baby and picked her up from the floor where Angela had put her. When he did, urine ran out of her diaper on to the kitchen floor and the stench of poop permeated the air.

"When did you change this baby last, Angela?" Marcus asked disgusted as he lay her back down on his kitchen floor and started taking off her diaper to see how bad the mess was. She had urine and runny poop oozing out the legs of her diaper as well as around the waistline.

"Yesterday, maybe . . . I don't remember." She replied making no effort to help him.

"Damn you Angela, this baby is totally raw from the waist down from diaper rash."

The baby screamed and turned red faced as he wiped off what filth he could. Removing all her clothes, he left her lying on the kitchen floor till he could run his kitchen sink full of warm water. Then he picked her up, holding her at arm's length and then placed her in the warm water and bathed her, forgetting he was suppose to be on his way to pick up Naomi. The baby relaxed in the comfort of the warm water and Marcus's gentle hands.

"Where is your diaper bag? Marcus asked as he finished bathing the baby. "Hand me a diaper."

"I didn't bring a bag. Diapers are a waste of money. Pin a tea towel on her." She replied.

Marcus shook his head in disgust and bit his lip. He then glanced over at Mary who was three and saw that she was equally as dirty.

"Adam, when you are finished eating, I want you to go get in my shower. Leave your clothes in the floor there. I will wash them so you can have them later. Grab one of my T-shirts from my closet and put it on. Make sure you shampoo your hair and use soap, do you understand?"

Adam didn't answer, but left the table and headed back to the master bathroom to do as Marcus said.

After wrapping the baby in a couple of tea towels, one for a diaper and one for a blanket, he placed her on the carpet till he could clean up Mary.

"The least you can do is fill the baby's bottle with milk and give it to her," He stated running another kitchen sink of warm water to clean Mary up in.

"There isn't any milk." She replied still digging in her big purse for something.

"What do you mean there is no milk?"

"I drank it, duh . . ." She replied.

"You drank the milk knowing your baby would need it!" He replied totally disgusted.

"Put some soda or beer in her bottle. She will be okay." She replied pulling what looked like newspaper engagement clipping from her huge purse.

Marcus once more bit his lip. His sister was unbelievable white trash. He undressed three year old Mary, letting her filthy clothes fall on to his kitchen floor. He was appalled when she removed her underwear. They looked like she had worn them for at least, a month. She had a rash just like the baby and had peanut butter and jelly in her matted hair that looked like it had been there for at least a week. It was going to take more than shampoo to get it out. Plus, she visibly had head lice. He shivered at the thought of the lice. He would have to clean everything the kids had come in contact with. Taking his dish liquid, he carefully scrubbed Mary's head being careful to not get it in her eyes. Then he bathed her in the dish liquid. She had crusted dirt and food on her. That was the breaking point for him. It took three sinks of water to clean three year old Mary up. He had always bailed his sister out when social services were up in arms wanting to take her children. If Adam, Mary, and Martha had any chance at life, they had to be taken away from Angela now. He didn't want them adopted out by social services to never be seen again. They were family. It was time to approach her about letting him adopt them. All thoughts of Naomi left him.

"I found it!" Angela stated as he dried Mary off with a tea towel. When he stood her down on the kitchen floor, she hugged his knee. He could see in her eyes that she was glad to be with him.

"Run and tell Adam to give you one of my T-shirts to put on. You can wear it till I wash your clothes."

Mary did as she was told and ran off naked toward the back bedroom.

"Angela, you and I have got to have a serious talk about the kids." He stated as all thoughts of Naomi and their walk by the river were forgotten.

"Let me show you this first." She stated handing him a wrinkled, newspaper clipping. "The kids can wait."

Marcus smoothed the tattered, wrinkled, clipped piece of newspaper out and was surprised to see that it was a wedding announcement.

"Surprise . . . !" Angela squealed.

Marcus read the clipping with disgust. "Isn't this a little late in coming. You have three kids and a fourth on the way. I would be embarrassed to have my friends and family see this. The picture is a cheap snapshot of you and Joe in a bar. I definitely don't want Jenkins or any of my friends seeing it. The least you could have done was have a decent photo made for the paper."

"Do you have Jenkins squirming on your hook again?"

"I was with her so long; her name, popping out of my mouth, just seems to happen sometimes. No, I am not seeing her. Why did you put a bar photo in the newspaper. Mom is not going to be happy about it or clip it for the family album."

"You and mom are just alike. My life doesn't fit in with your perfect little religious and social worlds, so you put me down. Can't you be just a little happy for me? I want you at my wedding. That is why I am here. Also, you will be proud of me. I called and asked Mom and Dad to come."

"If mom and dad come, Angela, you had better show them some respect or I will get up and walk out taking them with me. Do you understand?" He retorted.

"Don't get your undershorts in a wad. They will get the respect they deserve."

"Is mom going to preside as minister and marry the two of you?" He asked knowing how appalled his mother had to be.

"I asked her and she told me no, which didn't surprise me. She said she would come to my wedding, but she would not ask God to condone my sins. She has shut me out just like she always did when I was at home. I don't fit her pious, little mold of how a woman should live."

"She has a reason for turning you down, Angela. She sees thru Joe and his years of empty promises. She doesn't buy his lies about being a traveling sales man who sells tattoo supplies. You have never seen any of his earnings, but I imagine you have given him plenty of money over the years that should have gone for clothes and other items for your kids. You are a hooker, Angela, selling yourself for money for him. Mom knows and she isn't condoning it."

"Well, things are going to change now. We are getting married and we will have one child, buy a house in the suburbs of Nashville or St. Louis, and be respectable just like you."

Marcus was seething at her lack of concern for the outcome of Adam, Mary, and Martha. He thought about Mary and how she had hugged his leg like he was the only one that had ever loved her.

"How did you convince Joe to marry you . . . ?" He asked in disgust.

"We were separated for most of last year. He moved to St. Louis. He called wanting to come back home. You would have been proud of me, I gave him an ultimatum. If he wanted to come back, he had to agree to marry me. I stood my ground and demanded he buy me a big house like yours. I told him not to come home unless he had the down payment for one. However, I told him that I was willing to hook and make the house payments."

"You think forcing him to marry you will make your problems go away? Vows are just words, Angela. Vows only mean something when two partners are committed to each other. You have told me on many occasions that you have suspected Joe of cheating on you with multiple other women. A man doesn't disappear for months, if he loves you. You are just finances to him, Angela! I dare say he has a woman elsewhere that has thrown him out and once again he needs what little is in your purse to survive."

"Please, Marcus, be happy for me. I love him and I promise to take good care of his baby. I plan to name it Abraham, after Joe's father. If it is a girl, Joe wants to name it Naomi, after a cousin of his. I will dump the other three with social services immediately after my wedding on Saturday. I need the welfare check that comes on them next Friday to pay for the rent on the wedding chapel and the minister's fee. I honestly am just asking you to take them for just this week till I get my hands on my welfare check and our food stamps. I need the food stamps to buy the food items for my reception. Saturday evening, when the wedding is over, I plan to march the three up to the county offices' doors and leave them."

"There is only one way that I will take Adam, Mary, and Martha for the next week. You sign papers tonight relinquishing all parental rights, giving me full custody and adoption rights stating that their fathers are Johns, and that you don't want them. Otherwise, I am telling you to take them back home with you and I am walking out that door and going to my Lady friend's apartment and not returning. Do you understand me?" He stated mad.

Marcus glanced at baby Martha who was hungry and without diapers, yet his sister was thinking of spending her food stamps on wedding reception food. He suddenly saw her for what she was. She wasn't being a sister to him or a mother to them. His mother had tried to tell him over the years that she was self-centered white trash.

"Why would you want the three little bastards? They have been a noose around my neck as well as yours." She retorted.

"They are family, Angela."

"Take them if you want them. It isn't a problem with me. Just don't ever bring them to my new home in the suburbs. I don't want to have to explain to my respectable new neighbors who they are." She stated pausing for a moment and then continued. "However, you will have to agree to let me have Mary and Adam for an hour next Saturday and your rights to them doesn't start till after I receive my check and stamps next Friday. Adam is going to be the ring bearer and Mary the flower girl at my wedding. I have already bought their outfits. After that, I don't care if I ever see them again. They have been a drag." She replied.

Marcus bit his lip and pulled his cell phone from his jeans pocket and rang his attorney's number asking him to make an exception and open up his office after hours for some paperwork explaining the situation. His attorney, Tony Beale, agreed to do so at double time rates. It was the weekend. Then Marcus rang his neighbor, Mrs. Akins, and asked her if she would sit with the three kids while he ran and signed adoption papers. She agreed, if it was only for an hour or so.

Thoughts of Naomi had escaped Marcus in the hype of the moment. He was finally rescuing his nieces and nephew from his sister and the gutter they had lived in.

At the attorney's office, Marcus explained all the facts to Tony.

"So, Miss Bates, to start with, why do you go by the name of Bates when your legal name is Plum?"

"I ran away from home when I was fifteen. I felt I needed a new identity to hide from my parents. I passed a mortuary by that name as I was hitchhiking and took it for my new last name. After two or three years, it just became who I was."

"You will have to sign the paperwork with that name as well as your legal birth name of Plum." He stated making a note of the two names. "Am I to understand also, that on all three of your children's birth certificates, no father's names are listed?"

"I am a prostitute, and a damn good one. All three of my kids are accidents by Johns. They have no fathers."

"You are willing to sign paperwork stating that, in order to give Marcus full custody as well as no problems in court?"

"Yes."

"You are giving Marcus immediate guardianship starting now with a couple of minor requests for next Saturday when the two oldest of your children will participate in your wedding, is that correct?"

"If Marcus doesn't take them, I plan to dump them next Saturday night into the foster care system and let them be adopted out."

Marcus bowed his head in embarrassment at his sister's cold attitude toward her children.

"Alright, the two of you sit still. There are magazines on the table behind you. It will take my secretary about thirty minutes to type up all the paperwork involved. You do know, Angela, your children will belong totally to Marcus, once you sign the papers. You will never have any say so as to his care for them or how he chooses to raise them. They are his when you sign the paperwork."

"I am a big girl, Mr. Beale. I know what I want and it is not them. I have never wanted them."

At eight-thirty, Marcus and Angela signed the paperwork. Marcus wrote the attorney a check, using Naomi's engagement ring money, to pay for his services and they left.

Outside the attorney's office, Marcus breathed a sigh of relief. He had finally managed to get Adam, Mary, and Martha away from his sister and Joe. Now they stood a chance in life. He glanced at his watch. It was nine.

"Oh God . . . !" He muttered as he suddenly remembered Naomi. She was going to be one mad, pissed off Amish woman. She had made a point of telling him how important the evening was to her. He tried to ring Karen, but apparently she was still drunk and not answering her phone. By the time he took Angela to the bus station, stopped to buy diapers, milk, cereal, and head lice shampoo, it would be at least ten o'clock. Naomi was going to be irate with him as well as not speak to him for who knew how long. He was in one major dog house, not to mention he was going to have to tell her that he had adopted Adam as well as his two sisters.

Pulling up in front of the bus station, Marcus gave Angela cash for a bus ticket back and said in parting, "Now, Sis, you understand the terms. You are not to come back here to my house till the kids turn eighteen. It isn't that I don't love you. I want to raise them as their father, not their Uncle Marcus."

"This is one of the happiest nights of my life, Marcus. I am free from the three John bastards and I am marrying the man I love in a week."

"I will be there for your wedding next week. After that, you and Joe are on your own. I hope things work out the way you want them to. However, no matter how your life turns out, you cannot return to my house in Paducah for any reason. It makes me sad to have to say this to you, Angela, but my prediction is that Joe will run off again with who knows who within three months. He is using you again. Stop and think about how many tricks he has probably asked you to turn since returning? You are temporary finances to him."

"He is saving the money for new furniture for our house. He has it all tucked away safely in one hundred dollar bills in his billfold."

"You are so naïve." Marcus muttered knowing that someday, he would have a fourth child to adopt. His dreams of having children of his own were shot to Hell.

Arriving home, close to eleven, he apologized to Mrs. Atkins explaining the paperwork took longer than planned and showed it to her so that she wouldn't think he had lied about it. She immediately left not smiling, handing him Martha diapered in another set of tea towels. He knew within himself that Mary and Adam had probably been mouthy, holy terrors. He tried once more to ring Karen, but to no avail. The evening was what it was, shot! He poured milk into a new baby bottle and then sat down on the couch with Martha to feed her. As he did, he heard Naomi's words ringing in his ears, "Tonight is important to me, Marcus. Don't be late."

In the invisible, Frankie Frances and Osceola Black Lightning watched as

Naomi and Jack returned to his apartment after moving out of hers. After they ate at the steak house, they got prints made from the photos Naomi took of Karen and Marcus at the bistro. Naomi thumb tacked a photo of Karen having her hand on Marcus' pants fly to her front door and slipped one under Karen's door just before Jack loaded the last of her few things into the trunk of his car. Her life in Paducah had ended a week quicker than she had planned.

In the invisible, Osceola and Frankie Frances watched.

"Is she really going to spend the night in Jack's apartment, bed, and arms?" Frankie Frances asked in her honey dipped voice as she watched Jack make himself a bed on the couch while Naomi spread her new someday quilt on Jack's bed. "You did give her that dream last spring about her and Jack making love. We are going to be separating a couple of bed jumpers!" Frankie Frances stated holding her eye glasses in place and hoping to get to watch something interesting for a change.

"Get your mind out of the gutter, Frankie Frances. God pairs and it is not our duty to keep Naomi and Jack apart, if they should decide to do a little bed jumping, as you put it. We are guardian angels at the present, not cupids."

"If I was a cupid angel, I would shoot a love arrow straight into her and Dan Maynard's heart. They are more suited for each other. He is rich, handsome, has employees to boss around, and probably has a huge house out in the suburbs. Naomi would probably have a huge kitchen and the finest of pans to bake her breads in. I would then be rewarded by God for being Heaven's number one matchmaker."

"You would match Naomi with any good looking hunk that doesn't have pimples on his face. Love isn't about being paired with a handsome man. Love is mutual respect between two individuals and the putting of each other first. Jack is like my long legged Rabbit man. He has arms to hold you and not expect anything from you, unless you are willing. If anyone is a bed jumper, it will be our Naomi. I gave the love dream to her." Osceola Black Lightning replied in her syrupy fly swatting voice.

"I say it will be Jack that heads for her bed." Frankie Frances replied.

"Put up or shut up . . . what do you want to bet?" Osceola asked in her syrupy voice.

"If I win, you give me your nail file sword." Frankie Frances stated smiling in confidence from ear to ear.

153

"What if I win? I am not interested in your jar of pimple crème." Osceola retorted.

"If you win, Ms. Osceola Black Lightning, I will go back to Heaven, forget about being a guardian angel, and resume my duties as a dog walker."

Osceola broke out in a huge grin. This was her chance to get rid of her nemesis. She hated being stuck with the young, mouthy, angel who was driving her crazy.

"If Naomi makes her way to Jack's bed, you will return to Heaven and I will never have to look at you again?"

"Yes . . . and if Jack heads for Naomi's bed, I get your nail file sword." Frankie Frances stated in her Honey dipped, young southern voice just sure that she would be the winner.

"You do know that God will discipline us when we get home for gambling on the job?" Osceola asked all grins with a plan forming in her head.

"The most the White Suit can do to me is to give me an extra dog or two to walk. I am Heaven's number one dog walker. Walking a couple extra dogs will be a piece of cake. However, the Big Man is likely to discipline you by taking away your leave to go see your long legged Jack Rabbit man."

"I am willing to take my chances." Osceola replied all smiles. "However, you are wrong about what God could discipline you with. He could discipline you by never letting you lay your eyes again on that handsome young angel named Corky that your heart was racing for earlier. Should he be your soul mate, you won't be making love to anyone for eternity."

"I won't tell about our bet, if you don't." Frankie Frances stated smiling from ear to ear and sure that she would be the winner.

So, the two angels stood in the middle of the huge, one room loft apartment and watched. Jack stepped out on to the balcony till Naomi had a chance to undress and get in bed. Then he entered and went into the bathroom to undress and put his pajamas on. Then, he lay down on the couch. Two hours passed and both Naomi and Jack fell asleep.

"Well, this is a bummer, neither one of them is going to be a bed jumper." Frankie Frances stated bored to tears with her glasses slid down onto the end of her nose. They continued to stand in the middle of the dark apartment keeping an eye on Jack and Naomi.

Osceola pulled out her long nail file and began to work on her nails. Frankie Frances ignored her. That was what Osceola wanted. When her assistant wasn't looking, she swished her nail file sword giving Naomi an urge to have to get up and go pee. Within five minutes, Naomi threw back her quilt and swung her legs and feet around and onto the floor. Jack was snoring, so Naomi didn't bother to wrap a quilt or anything around her white Amish night gown. She had to walk past the back of the couch in order to go to the rest room.

"No . . . no . . . no . . ." Frankie Frances stated scurrying to step in front of Naomi. She waved her hands frantically in front of Naomi trying to stop her. "Go back . . . go back, wait for Jack to be the jumper!"

Naomi walked right thru the invisible Frankie Frances and instantly shivered, thinking that there was a chill in the apartment.

Just as Naomi stepped behind the couch where Jack slept, Osceola gave a quick little swish and sway with her nail file sword seeing that Frankie Frances was not looking at her. Naomi tripped and fell over the back of the couch landing on top of Jack who was instantly awake and in shock.

Frankie Frances, in the invisible, instantly went to crying and trying to pull Naomi off the top of Jack.

"I win, Ms. Frankie Frances." Osceola Black Lightning stated in a jubilant, syrupy, sticky fly swatting voice. "Pack your pimple crème, you are going home."

"You tricked me into gambling. I am going to tell God on you, Ms. Osceola black Lightning. You caused me to sin."

Then they were interrupted by the voice of Jack.

"What are you doing on top of me?" Jack asked putting his arms around Naomi to keep her from rolling off and hurting herself. She seemed off balanced.

"What are you doing under me?" Naomi asked aware that she was skimpily dressed and on top of the man she had fantasized about last spring.

"Do you walk in your sleep?" Jack asked in shock, not releasing her. Naomi in his arms was a moment that he had dreamed about.

"Apparently, I do. Now, I will have to marry you when I am free to make an honest man out of you. I am really sorry, Jack. I have defiled your arms."

"Is that a promise, Naomi?" He asked suddenly laughing as he held her on top of him with his arms wrapped securely around her.

"May I kiss you just once, Jack? I wish to know if your kiss is as good as it is in my dreams. I have dreamed about being in your arms."

"You have?" He asked in shock.

"Yes, last spring I had a night dream and I was in your arms, in your bed, and you made love to me. I do not know how I have managed to end up on top of you, but your arms feel really good and I would very much like to kiss you."

"Well, Sweet Thing, as much as I love you and want you, I know you will hate yourself if you make love to me before your divorce. I am turning your kiss down. I will wait."

Naomi grinned looking down at him. "I am safe in your arms. That is something I have never known."

"You will always be safe with me, Naomi. I will never abuse you or take advantage of you. Should I make love to you one day, I want it to be special. Now, I am going to reluctantly unwrap my arms from around you and I assume you are going to be a lady and remove yourself from on top of me."

Naomi put her hand on the side of Jack's face. "I know you will be the only one left standing with me after Joel is arrested. I am sorry that my heart raced for Marcus. It should have raced for you."

"I am willing to wait for your heart to race for me. I am a patient man and besides, you are going to have to make an honest man out of me now. You have been in my couch bed."

"Indeed I have been." She replied. "There is no need for you to sleep on this couch now. We will share the bed and put pillows down the center to keep us apart. I will check your patience." She stated laughing and rolling off the top of him.

Jack sat up grinning. "Do I get the right or left side?"

"God is my right hand friend, so I guess you get the left." She replied.

"The left it is." He replied sitting up and then standing. He then swept her up in his arms and carried her to the bed and placed her on the right side. He then circled the bed and got in on the left side placing one of the pillows between them.

Pulling her someday quilt upon him, he stated. "Good night, Sweet Thing! You are safe with me."

Naomi reached over the pillow and placed her hand on his chest. "Good night, Jack. You and I are sleeping beneath my someday quilt. I promise you I will never share it with anyone but you."

He took her hand and raised it to his lips and kissed it. "I love you, Naomi."

"When I am over grieving for Marcus, I will love only you forever. I know you are my someday man."

CHAPTER THIRTEEN

Begging for Help

Having set his alarm clock, Marcus rose at six a.m. to catch his mother while she was cooking breakfast before church. He needed help and he couldn't think of anyone else to ask on a weekend. His university friends were not answering their phones. Karen was drunk and Jack wasn't the baby sitting type. Jenkins he didn't dare call, short of losing Naomi forever.

Since leaving home after high school, he had distanced his-self from his mother and her fanatical religious beliefs. He kept his Paducah life as much a secret from her as possible, including who he dated. All the married women he had been with, he now regretted. He always saw them as safe or as finances for his college and then master's degree program. His parents had not paid for his education. He had distanced himself from them and that included any finance ties. He felt like garbage now that he had met Naomi. He wished he had waited for Naomi to come along as well as financed his education in a different manner. His mother had been right in some of her demands on him as a teen.

Marcus' mother was a Holiness Pentecostal minister. She preached hell hot, fornication a sin, and a strict, holiness dress code. It was the dress code and the holiness that got him. He had wanted to join the school swim team when he was in high school. His mother refused to let him, stating that the exposing of your body for women or girls to look at in clothing that was skimpy like underwear was sin. He had never forgiven her for it and did join the college swim team when he left home. He had swimming trophies his parents had never seen and he had created a secret life in Paducah that did not measure up to his parent's holiness standard. His three year love affair with the beautiful, blonde, married Professor Jenkins was one of several affairs he had as rebellion against who he once was. Now, Naomi had come along and everything he had done, in the form of rebellion, was coming back to nip him in the butt. He was in love with a woman with standards who was just like his mother. Naomi now knew about Jenkins and she had been a source of contention between them. Naomi suspected his other affairs with older women, but so far one of them hadn't gotten in Naomi's face like Jenkins had.

Marcus waited for his mother to pick up the phone.

"Plum residence, Rev. Rachael Plum speaking . . ." His mother answered.

"Morning Mom," Marcus greeted her while wondering how he was going to dare ask her to come spend a few days and babysit for him.

"It has been awhile. Are you okay?" She asked.

"I know it has been awhile and I am sorry, believe me. I have called to ask you for a favor."

"What is it?" She asked simply.

"Angela is marrying Joe. She brought the kids to me last night and has signed papers letting me adopt them. As of this morning, I am a father. Adam, Mary, and Martha are mine. Angela signed the adoption papers last night. I could use a little help for two or three days till I get a schedule worked out and go purchase clothes and things for them. Would you consider coming to Paducah for two or three days?" He inquired, hating having to ask.

"I can't come, Marcus. I have invited a lady friend to come spend a few days with me. She is coming by bus and will be here tonight. We have had this time together planned for several weeks. She is holiness like me and the visit between us is important. We have a lot to pray about together and discuss. I cannot come."

"You are choosing to visit with some fruitcake church friend instead of helping me with your grandchildren?" He shot back in not too nice of a tone.

"Yes, that is my choice; just as you have made a choice to take Angela's bastard children. You should have planned ahead for childcare and what you need. A responsible parent does that."

"How can you be that cold to me and your grandchildren?"

"Your father and I have taken a hands-off approach, where Angela is concerned. We have put her on the altar and left her there. We have better things to do with our time than to aid you and her in your sins. Angela has chosen to become white trash. We are not condoning her sin or helping her raise white trash children. I know that sounds harsh, but it is our decision. We have Sunday school children who need us and are appreciative of our interaction with them. Angela appreciates nothing and has raised her children to do the same. She has chosen to raise gutter rats and we will not crawl into the gutter with them. Apparently, you have once more run to her aid and swooped up her little heathen and have once more put your life on hold for them. The only hope Angela's children has is that social services steps in and takes them and adopts them out. That is what I and my holiness lady friend are praying for."

"We are family, mom. Angela, Adam, Mary, Martha, you, dad, and I are family. I can't let strangers have Angela's children and never see them again."

"No, you are mistaken. Your father, my lady friend, and I are family. I haven't seen you in two years and it was three years before that. You only live a couple hundred or so miles from me. Family comes home to Sunday dinner at least once a month. You and Angela abandoned us years ago because of our stand for holiness. My new lady friend, who is an orphan your age, comes home to your father and me and never fails to keep in touch."

"Angela and I are not replaceable, mom. Whoever the woman is, that you are singing her praises, is probably a con artist out to rip you and dad off." Marcus replied angrily, knowing that he had used at least twenty married women's money to pay for his slide thru college and then his master's degree program.

"Yes, you are replaceable. When Job lost everything including his children in the bible, God replaced them." His mother retorted. "I lost you when you left home after high school. Now, God has replaced you and Angela and given me a daughter who respects who I am and my values."

Marcus bit his lip. He hated being preached to.

"I don't want to hear the new daughter crap, Mom! Angela and I are not replaceable and one day you will regret your words." Marcus shot back. Calming his voice he then asked. "Are you attending Angela's wedding?"

"Yes, but I am not taking a camera. I am going for one reason only."

"What is that?" He asked.

"I want you to meet my lady friend. I feel she is right for you. God sent her our way and she is everything to me that Angela isn't. She prays, quilts with me, and respects my views concerning holiness. She is the daughter I have always dreamed of having. She walks and talks with God like me. Henry is just as crazy about her. When she visits, she drives one of his farm implements and helps in the fields. I know God has sent her here because she is the one for you."

"Forget the dreams, mom. I am not marrying some uneducated, member of your cult."

"Someday, Marcus, God is going to bend and break you for your disrespect of me as a minister and the path I have chosen. God will either let you come down with some illness that you can't find healing for, or you will lose the one thing you love the most. When God avenges the righteous, he is a fierce task master. Your time of tears and bended knees are coming, Marcus. My lady friend is a child of God and respectable. I have turned your sister over to God and in this moment I am doing the same with you. I have had my fill of your disrespect."

"You are a hypocrite mom. You are disrespecting your grandchildren by throwing them away like garbage." He stated ignoring her warning and the cult fruitcake she was trying to fix him up with.

"Die, sink, or swim, we have put Angela on the altar and are leaving her there. She is on her own and in God's hands. She is an adult woman who needs to face the consequences of what she does and the hell she has created for others and her children. I am a Heaven going person and my feet are planted on holy ground. I will not walk in Hell with her or you by baby sitting her little hellions. I have washed my hands of her and my grandchildren, as you call them."

"So, as usual you are leaving me to pick up the pieces for our family." He smirked.

"You don't pick up anything, Mark. You are a dumping ground for Hell's waste. You have always been your sister's patsy. She cons you for your savings and weeks of free childcare. You have always under-minded our stand for tough love with her. You aid her in her sins. She would have lost the kids long ago to social services, if you hadn't kept picking up the pieces hiring her lawyers and paying for them. Without you, she would have had to face the real world, got a job, went back to school, and possibly made better choices for herself. Once more, you have stepped up to the plate and taken her garbage that she doesn't want to take responsibility for. She is foot loose and fancy free running around Nashville this morning, while you are struggling to find baby sitters. You will raise her gutter rats and be there when she has more to dump on you. Hear my word, son, God does repay sin and those like you who embrace the sinners. Angela will eventually reap by losing that which she loves the most and you will probably lose your chance for being with the right woman and having a family of your own. You have embraced Angela's sins and now you are paying for them this morning. I will not embrace my daughter and her sins, nor will I help you the embracer. You embraced her three sins willingly, you figure out what to do with them. I have to go."

"Are you telling me to die, sink, or swim mom?" He asked pissed.

"It is harsh, but yes. The only chance those kids have for a normal life is if they are adopted out separately to strangers. I have washed my hands of Angela and that includes her children. You are fooling yourself if you think Angela is going to just walk away. She will waltz back into your life down the road, suing your for custody when she realizes she no longer has food stamps, housing, and a welfare check when Joe dumps her or disappears again. Your problems have only just begun. If you had stayed out of her life and let our tough love work years ago, her kids would already be adopted out and well on the way to becoming someone as children. You have linked yourself to a gutter rat and have enabled her to take three little rats down into the sewer's darkness with her."

Marcus hung up on his mother, a first for him and one which he would regret. He would eventually see that his mother was right.

Begging every friend he had, Marcus finally came up with a teen sitter for Adam and Mary. It was Sunday noon. Nervous about standing Naomi up, mad at his mother, and toting a crying baby, Marcus headed for Naomi's place. He didn't know how to explain the baby he was toting. If he told her now that he had adopted Angela's three kids, she would very likely dump him. His only hope was to tell her that he was baby sitting for the day and let her bond with the baby. He could keep the kids hidden out across town at his place for a month or two. His main concern was apologizing and coming up with a good excuse for standing her up. He knew he was in a serious dog house.

Arriving at the apartment complex, he parked in front along the curb and got the baby and her carrier out. This was a sprinting up the three floors to apologize morning, but with a baby in tow, he climbed carefully. As he did so, he noticed that there was something thumb tacked to her door up above. It looked like a photo of some sort.

Twisting and turning, he finally reached the top and after a step or two across the third floor landing he faced Naomi's door and in shock almost dropped the carrier that the baby was in. He quickly jerked the photo down. It was a photo of him and Karen in front of the bistro and it was of the moment when Karen had drunkenly run her hand down the fly of his trousers.

"Oh God, no . . ." Marcus gasped.

Immediately, he began pounding on Naomi's door knowing what the photo looked like. There was no way Naomi was going to believe his plumber story or any other story as to why he had stood her up. He knew she was thinking that he was having an affair and had stood her up for Karen.

"It had to be Jack that took the photo." Marcus muttered in a pissed off mood.

He pounded some more, but there was no answer. In desperation, he took his foot and just kicked the door open. He could not put off this confrontation with her or he would lose her. He would just have to tell her the truth about the adoption of the kids and ask his attorney to vouch for where he was last evening. Surely, Karen would corroborate his story, once she was sober.

The door crashed open after he kicked it. "Naomi . . ." He yelled. She didn't answer. He entered the apartment after picking the baby and her carrier up. To his surprise, the apartment was empty. What few things that Naomi owned were gone including her rolling tote, baking pans, and pallet from the closet.

"Damn it . . . damn it . . . damn it!" He cursed wondering where she could have moved so quickly in the middle of the night.

Taking the baby, he hurried back out of the apartment and then down the stairs intending to pound on Karen's door and see if she had a confrontation with Naomi and possibly knew where she had gone. The only other option was Jack's place. He had to of taken the photo.

"Some hell of a friend he has turned out to be!" He muttered as he made his way to the manager's unit.

Standing in front of Karen's apartment, he pounded but she didn't come to the door. He peeked in her front window and saw that she was passed out on her couch. He was not going to get any information, concerning the whereabouts of Naomi, from her. Getting back into his jeep, after buckling the baby and her carrier in, he headed for Jack's place, a second floor loft apartment overlooking the street and the bistro. As he drove, the ramblings of drunken Karen played in his head. He thought about the gold safety pin and her insinuation that Jack was in love with Naomi, not her.

"Damn him! He caught my guard down and moved in on me." Marcus muttered mad.

Parking by the curb in front of Jack's building; he took a deep breath to calm him-self. He was going to have to confront his best friend. They had gone thru high school, college, and all of life afterward together. They were two farm boys who went off to explore the world and seek their fortunes together. Now, a woman had come between them. Marcus once more got the baby and her carrier out. He then looked up at the balcony in front of Jack's apartment. Naomi had told him that she was going to have an early burger with him. Surely, she wasn't up there last night standing and watching. That was a horror thought. His arms had been all over Karen and his red haired drunken friend had all but raped him in public. Hopefully it was just Jack that saw the display. He could somehow explain away the photo, if he thought hard enough.

After he climbed to the third floor balcony, he took a good look down at the sidewalk in front of the bistro. There was no doubt in his mind that his best friend Jack had taken the photo and given it to Naomi. Mad, he turned, sat the baby and her carrier down on the balcony floor, and pounded on Jack's loft apartment door. After a few moments of heavy duty knocking, a sleepy eyed Jack opened the door.

"Where is Naomi?" Marcus demanded red faced. "I know you took the photo of Karen and me and then stabbed me in the back by giving it to Naomi. Where is she?"

"It is a little early to be making demands on me!" Jack retorted rubbing his face with his hands.

"It is noon and why in the hell would you give Naomi that photo. You know I am in love with her." Marcus spouted. Martha started crying due to the sudden sound of their harsh voices.

"I printed the photo, but I didn't take it. Your fooling Naomi days are over, pal. She didn't have to see the photo; she was standing up here on the balcony waiting for me and saw you and Karen below. She took my camera and took the photos after spotting you and Karen coming up the sidewalk with Karen in your arms. I believe you told her that you were going to be late due to entertaining a plumber and his wrenches. Naomi took the photo you saw and left it on her apartment door so that you and my red head would know that she saw the two of you. Karen's hand down the front of your trousers was the breaking moment for Naomi. You and Karen have played a fast one. In case you have forgotten, Karen is supposed to be my girlfriend. I honestly didn't see your blindside coming, pal. Your playing around with my red head was a shocker. She is history to me this morning."

"There is nothing between Karen and me."

"Naomi and I stood here and watched the two of you kiss, as well as have your hands all over each other. Karen is history and you are probably the same with Naomi."

"You are dumping Karen?"

"I will not be seeing Karen anymore. However, I once told you that should you dump or get dumped by Naomi, I was going to make her my girl. Last night was important to her and you screwed yourself. Now, it is my turn to chase her. Unlike you, I won't be having any after hour plumbing wenches to have to explain. After her divorce, she is mine."

"You are a back stabbing traitor of a friend. You know that I am in love with Naomi."

"I have not had to back stab you. Naomi was up here on the balcony waiting on me to take her down to the Bistro for a burger. You should have been home with a plumber like you told her. Naomi is a black and white person. There are no shades of gray with her."

"What about the pin, Jack. I am ripping that damn, two thousand dollar safety-pin off her dress, when I see her. She is my girl. I am not giving up."

"Well, she has worn the same pair of shoes for two years with duck tape on the bottom. If she is your girl, you should be seeing to her needs, not your sister's. Naomi took care of me for six weeks when I had surgery last winter and wouldn't take a dime for it. She deserves every damn dollar I spent on that pin as well as the new shoes she has on, and a lifetime of my devotion to her. She was there for me when I had no one. She walked everyday to see me in the snow and helped me on and off bedpans and emptied urinals when I barely knew her. I don't recall you, my friend, doing anything but calling me once on the phone. You have been my best friend since high school. When the chips were down and I needed a friend, it was Naomi who stepped up to the plate. I will do anything for her including saving her from you, if I have to. When you can match the gift of the safety pin and shoes; then talk to me. You take from women, not give to them. The only woman that ever gets anything out of you is your damn sister who always has her hand in your pocket."

Marcus cringed at Jack's words. He knew Jack was right. He had taken Naomi's engagement ring money and used it to adopt his sister's kids. Jack was a friend who had always told him like it was. He had indeed used women, till Naomi came along.

"Naomi is mine, Jack. Where is she?" Marcus asked in an angry huff. He was now mad at himself for not being there for Naomi. He had never given her shoes or clothing a second thought. He had indeed been funneling all his money down Angela and her kid's never ending money pit.

"Naomi is not yours! She could have been! Last night was important to her. You stood Naomi up and was seen kissing Karen. You lied to her about being with a plumber, and you got caught up with. You had your chance with Naomi and blew it. I owe Naomi and I will always put her and her needs first. You have too many married fish on your line, pal. Naomi has jumped off of your fishing hook and is gone. Your life as a gigolo is nipping you where it hurts. "

"It is unfair throwing the women of my past into this." Marcus sputtered.

"I am just saying that Naomi always comes in last with you." Jack replied glancing down at the bawling baby. "You are ignoring that baby! What are you doing with her, anyway?"

"She is why I couldn't get back to Naomi last night. My sister gave me custody and adoption rights last night. I was signing paperwork till way late in the evening. I tried calling Karen to ask her to give Naomi a message. She was drunk and wouldn't answer her phone."

"Well, did you think about calling me? Naomi was with me and you knew she was going with me for a burger. I do have a phone, Marcus."

"I didn't think about it." Marcus stated suddenly realizing he had made some very bad choices the night before.

"That is just it, Marcus. You don't think, not about Naomi. Adopting three kids without her knowing is a good example."

"We are supposed to be friends, Jack. Be a friend and back off from Naomi. Naomi and I will work it out concerning these kids."

"I will never back off from Naomi. She was there for me when I needed her and I will always be there watching her backside. She is still trying to save the money for headstones for her dead children. She needs someone to hold her and make her feel safe, not make a nurse maid out of her."

"Naomi and I are meant to be together. She will understand about these kids, after I explain to her."

"Good luck explaining them and kissing Karen. When you get thru explaining them, then start in on all the married women you have slept with including Jenkins for money."

"I want to know, Jack. Have you told Naomi about my days as a gigolo when I was working my way thru college?"

"I don't tell Naomi anything about you. I don't have to. I also haven't told her that you have been hitting the sheets to make money to buy her an engagement ring. Your secrets just seem to surface on their own. Sleeping with Jenkins again for money as well as Mavis' aunt and a handful of other married women around town are a little risky don't you think? Jenkins is sleeping with someone you are unaware of and you are likely to get a good dose of who knows what from her."

"Please don't tell Naomi. I have just been trying to come up with money for an engagement ring. Angela has drained me the last year and my savings are depleted. I only planned to hit the sheets long enough to get the ring, honest."

"Naomi was once her husband's doormat, but she is no man's rug now. Your adopting those kids is walking on her and that is how she will see it, if you can ever get her to speak to you again."

"Where is she Jack?" Marcus demanded unable to refute what his best friend had said. Jack always told him the truth about himself.

"She moved out of Karen's complex last night and stored her things with me. She is gone. I put her on a five A.M. bus to Missouri. She has walked out of our lives, just as she once walked into them."

"Damn you Jack!" Marcus spouted picking up the baby carrier with one mad crying baby in it. He quickly stuck a pacifier in her mouth. Then he hurried down the stairs wondering what he was going to do. He couldn't chase after Naomi with three kids in tow. His jeep could only handle one car seat and his neighbor teen baby sitter had agreed to only an hour and a half of services. That time was about up.

When he reached the ground level with the stairs emptying out into a side alley, he leaned against the building's wall, holding onto Martha's carrier, and burst into tears. How was he ever going to find her with three kids that he couldn't find sitters for? His knees felt like Jelly in fear that he had lost her. His mother's words were haunting him. He had indeed screwed up his life.

"Please God, don't take from me the thing I love the most, Naomi." He prayed as tears rolled down his handsome, distraught face.

CHAPTER FOURTEEN

Karen's Discovery

Later in the evening, Marcus found a second teen baby sitter and he loaded the baby and her carrier into his jeep. The baby was too young to trust to a teen. Mary and Adam were rowdy enough to hold their own with anyone. They would be fine with the neighbor's teen. Climbing into the driver's seat, he headed for Karen's place hoping she was sober. He had to find Naomi. Karen was going to have to tell her that it was her that came on to him in her drunken state, not him her. He had never had to explain himself to a woman before and hardly knew where to start with Naomi. Naomi wasn't like other women. She was as Jack told him, black and white in her thinking and no in-between shades of gray.

Marcus was still wearing the same clothes from the night before. He had fallen asleep on his couch with baby Martha in his arms. On awakening at seven in the morning, he had three kids to feed and find baby sitters for. Changing into different clothing or showering hadn't been high on his priorities' list. His number one priority had been to somehow find childcare for Adam and Mary so he could make his way to Naomi to apologize. His mother had turned him down as well as most of his neighbors. Those who had baby sat Adam and Mary, on previous stays with him, laughed and told him to dream on. Adam and Mary were undisciplined, holy terrors with no manners.

Reaching Karen's place, it was three in the afternoon. His sister's newspaper wedding announcement was hanging haphazardly out of his back pocket. He had stuck it there the previous evening to show his attorney. Climbing in and out of the jeep had caused it to start to work its way out of his back pocket.

Marcus peeped in the front window of Karen's apartment and saw that she was no longer on the couch. He knocked and nervously waited for her to open her door. After a moment or so, she did so. Her wild, red, frizzy red hair was not in its usual ponytail and she looked like a red haired clown with a bad hangover. She had a glass of tomato juice in one hand.

"May I come in? I need to talk to you." Marcus asked shuffling the baby's carrier handle from one hand to the other. "We have problems that you might not be aware of, yet."

"Oh . . . I am aware. I found a photo and the key to Naomi's apartment stuck under my door when I woke up an hour or so ago. Why was I at the bistro with you last night? Also, why were you holding me in your arms?" She asked guzzling her glass of tomato juice trying to sober up.

"You tied one on downtown and stumbled out onto the sidewalk as I was on my way to the bistro to pick up carry out. You were drunk as a skunk and doing some serious wobbling in your spikes. I caught you to keep you from falling and then walked you down to the bistro to pour some coffee down you. I am sorry about manhandling you, but you weren't standing on your own."

"Come on in. I don't remember a thing past three when my day of teaching was over yesterday. I seem to recall opening a bottle of vodka in my car and drinking straight from it. My next recollection is waking up about an hour ago and finding Naomi's key and the photo. I gather from the key and her moving out that she thinks there is something between the two of us."

"You don't remember anything?" Marcus asked as Karen reached out and took Martha in her carrier from him. She then proceeded to take the carrier and set it down in the middle of her living room carpet. She plopped down onto the floor and proceeded to remove Martha and lay her on the carpet to look her over. She loved babies but had never conceived in the ten years she was with her Joey.

"I must have tied a really good one on. Whose baby do you have? She sure is cute."

"The baby is the youngest of my sister Angela's three children. I signed adoption papers last night after I turned you over to a friend of yours at the bistro, who drove you home. I have been trying for years to get custody of my nephew and nieces. It happened last night. My sister brought them to me and signed papers letting me adopt them."

"Did I really have my hand on your fly?" She asked seeing a newspaper clipping of some sort fall from Marcus' pocket onto the carpet.

"I am afraid so. I was having trouble keeping you standing with both my arms around you. You had a set of roaming hands that I didn't have a third arm to control. I think you might have thought I was Jack. You also kissed me, patted my backside, and threw your arms around my neck like we were teens on a necking adventure."

"Who took the photo?" She asked pointing for him to take a seat on the sectional as she picked Martha up and started to cuddle her. She had no hopes of ever having children.

"Jack and Naomi were standing on the balcony of his apartment across from the bistro. Both of them saw you kiss me and you manhandling my fly and backside. We didn't see them, but they saw us. Naomi took the photo using Jack's camera."

"That doesn't surprise me. They are trying to turn the table. It is you and I that have been betrayed by them." Karen retorted and then talked baby gibberish to Martha.

"Jack helped Naomi move out last night. She has caught a bus back to Missouri. I have to know where her farm is, Karen. As soon as I can figure out childcare for my kids, I am going after her. I need you to tell her that you were drunk, not with me, and that it was not me fondling or kissing you. I need you to tell her that, or I have lost her forever."

"Returning to her farm in Missouri seems logical. She has money in her pocket now and her two children are buried there. She has been saving to buy them headstones. There is no telling where she will go from there. You had better go after her quick or my traitor of a boyfriend will beat you to it. Have I told you about the two thousand dollar gold safety pin he bought her and the twenty dollar cheap ass book he gave me for my birthday?"

"Yes, you were rambling on and on about it last night. I have got to find her, Karen. Please help me, I love her."

"Discovering that Jack paid mega bucks for a piece of jewelry for your Naomi caused me to climb in to a serious bottle last night. I was hoping for an engagement ring from him for my birthday. What I got, was the shaft." She stated reaching over and picking up the newspaper clipping off the carpet.

"That is mine; it must have dropped out of my back pocket. My sister is getting married in Nashville next Sunday afternoon. She gave me the clipping when she turned her kids over to me last night. After ten or so years, three kids and one on the way, and multiple breakups, her and her Joe are going to tie the knot. The clipping is their newspaper wedding announcement." Marcus stated holding out his hand for the clipping.

"May I read the clipping?" Karen asked holding on to it. "I love weddings and babies. I think every woman does."

"Sure, go ahead. However, don't judge me by the photo my sister chose to put in the paper. She has no taste." Marcus replied.

Karen turned the clipping over and took a look at the newspaper photo and then gasped and choked on her own saliva. Marcus jumped to her aid and held one of her arms in the air while slapping her on the back. After gasping, trying to breathe, turning red, and tears of shock running down her cheeks; she managed to clear her windpipe. She then jumped to her feet with the clipping still in her hand and then quickly read the announcement. Turning white as a sheet, she looked at Marcus with big eyes and her mouth hanging open. She was instantly sober.

"The buzz cut woman is your sister?" Karen asked in shock not smiling.

"Yes, the buzz cut is my sister. What is wrong, Karen?" Marcus asked realizing that Karen was trembling.

"Last night, I tried to drown myself in a bottle thinking that Naomi was my enemy. You have to be the one that has caused ripples in my divorcing Joey. How long have you been using me and Naomi to spy for your sister?"

"I don't know what you are referring to." Marcus stated holding out his hand for the newspaper clipping.

"Does this baby lying in my floor belong to the buzz cut in the newspaper clipping?"

"Yes . . . my sister has three children and a fourth on the way. Why?"

Karen looked down at the baby and backed up.

"You get that damn baby off my floor and out of here. How dare you bring her here! Get out Marcus and don't you ever come back. Your sister broke up my marriage. I walked in on her and my husband together down in Nashville." She stated quickly walking to the door and holding it open for him.

"You what?" He asked in shock picking up Martha and putting her back into her carrier.

"Your sister works in a damn nursing home, doesn't she?"

"Yes, part time. Why?"

"I went down to Nashville to visit a fellow teacher who had gone into a nursing home there. I walked into a room and saw your buzz cut sister and my husband Joey making love in a nursing home bed. Joe in this announcement is my Joey."

"Oh crap . . ." Marcus replied in shock himself. "I am sorry, Karen. Honest, I didn't know that your Joey is my sister's Joe!"

"Like hell you didn't! You have been spying on me for her. You are the person who has sabotaged my divorce proceeding. Get out of my apartment and don't let me ever see you step one foot on my property, much less bring one of her bastard children here. I am glad Naomi misinterpreted last night. It serves you right. I will never tell her any difference because you and your sister have stuck it to me. Now get out!"

Marcus picked up the carrier with Martha in it and walked to the door and stepped past Karen. She then slammed the door in his face. Biting his lip, he returned to his vehicle and strapped Martha in the passenger seat of his jeep. As he did so, he took a really good look at her. Then he closed the door and walked around his jeep and climbed in to the driver's seat and closed the door.

Marcus didn't start his vehicle up. He got lost in thought for a few minutes. Angela had just cost him Karen for a friend, and possibly Naomi. He lay his face down on his arms on the steering wheel with depression setting in. He had Angela's kids, but in the process had lost his circle of close friends and the only woman that he knew he would ever love. He was screwed.

CHAPTER FIFTEEN

Heading for Nashville

The week dragged by and there was no word from Naomi. On Friday evening, Marcus left Martha with Mrs. Atkins and headed for Nashville with the other two kids in a rental car. His two seated jeep wasn't kid friendly. In one week's time, his life had drastically changed. His jeep was now parked on his front lawn with a for sale sign on it. The money he planned to buy Naomi an engagement ring with was gone and there was a baby bed in his bedroom for Martha. His house was trashed from Adam and Mary running thru the place like wild Indians. He had circles around his eyes from walking the floors with Martha who had developed colic. His life suddenly wasn't so pleasant. Raising his nephew and nieces wasn't the happy little picture he had envisioned. Also, his mother's words haunted him. Angela had indeed cost him the one thing he loved the most, Naomi. If he hadn't gone for Bistro food for her, he would very possibly be sleeping in the arms of the woman he loved.

There was no more making hotel reservations for a king size bed and a Jacuzzi. Tonight it was a double bed motel room with a kitchenette so he could feed the kids. He was on a tight budget, because he was not now free at night to hit the sheets and make a little extra money if needed. His weekend in Nashville was not going to be a bachelor, carefree one. He hadn't broken Adam and Mary yet from their foul mouths or lack of social graces. He was dreading interacting with adults who didn't know him and would think he condoned their behavior. His life in one week had gone from first class Jacuzzi to a low class motel with no swimming pool one. He had never considered what he would have to give up to rear children. However, reality had set in and he was not happy with his new life. He knew if he was married to Naomi, they would have well behaved children and a good life. Mary and Adam were nightmares and almost beyond reprogramming. His mother was right, although he would never tell her so. Angela had finally sucked all of his life out of him.

After checking into the motel and getting Mary and Adam settled in front of the television, he gave his mother's hotel room a ring.

"Rev. Plum speaking," she answered.

"I have called to apologize for hanging up on you. I am an adult and it was not appropriate behavior on my part." He stated quickly thinking she might hang up on him.

"You are not the only one who has hung up on me over the years. I am a minister and I tell it like it is. Are you checked in to your room?" She asked.

"Yes, I am checked in to a double with Mary and Adam. The baby is with my neighbor back in Paducah."

"I have my lady friend with me. I invited her to come with me to Angela's wedding. I want you to meet her tomorrow. She got in on the bus yesterday. She is really nice and your age. I just know she is the right one for you, Mark. I can hardly wait for you to meet her."

"You have tried to match me up with every single woman in your church between the ages of sixteen and forty over the years. I am not interested. Besides, no woman is going to want me with three kids. I have a big family now."

"When you meet my lady friend, I am asking you to not tell her about the kids. You still have time to turn them over to social services and let them be adopted out."

"I get your drift, mom. However, I can't do that. I have bonded with Martha this week. She clings to me and cries if anyone tries to take her from me. She is definitely going to be a daddy's girl."

"Don't get attached to her. You are guaranteed it won't be six months till Angela waltzes back in and sues you for custody of her. You will spend your last dollar on lawyers and the kids will suffer not knowing whether they belong with you or her. You need to take them to social services now and turn them over to the state to be adopted while you have custody of them. If you don't, your life will never be your own again. It will belong to process servers, court dates, and attorneys."

"Damn it, mom, you don't know what you are asking me to do?"

"Watch your language!" She replied in a demanding voice and then continued. "That is where you are wrong, Mark. I am asking you to let the kids have a chance for a normal life with strangers where Angela will not be able to find them."

"They are family, mom. I can't turn them over to strangers."

"Well, then expect Joe and Angela to suck your finances till they are dry and your personal life until you don't have one. When Joe dumps Angela again, she will be on your doorstep wanting the kids back for housing, a check, and food stamps. You may be educated, Mark; but you are a blind fool. You are throwing your life away as well as that of those three kids."

"Let's not argue about this. Adam, Mary, and Martha are family and I am not giving them up."

"The woman that I am going to introduce you to could be your family. She is right for you and would raise respectable children, not little heathen like Angela has produced."

"Mom . . . I am just not into the holiness crowd you hang out with. The last thing I want is a Pentecostal holiness wife. That is who you are going to try to push off on me this weekend; isn't it?"

"Pretty close. She is not Pentecostal, but she is holiness. I just know she could straighten you up."

"She is going to save me, huh?" He asked rolling his eyes in disgust.

"I have known her for about two years and she is just like me. I am thinking of asking her to move here and be my assistant pastor. She is not afraid to tell people they are sinners. She has been speaking for me one Sunday a month and our church is always filled with standing room only when she speaks."

"Great! It is going to be a long weekend mom keeping up with two kids and your lady friend stalking me. Please don't seat me next to her at the reception."

"We are not going to the reception. Angela is holding it at a biker's bar.

Your father and I will not enter a hell hole, nor will my lady friend. I hope you keep Mary and Adam out of there. If you are going to be their father, you have got to make decisions as to what places are proper for them."

"Grabbing a piece of cake and paper cup of punch in a biker's bar is not going to hurt them. The reception will probably last no more than an hour."

"Sin is sin, whether it is one minute, one hour, or a whole evening sitting and getting drunk. I don't condone drinking, nor will we step inside and drink punch or eat cake from the hands of devils. My lady friend will not be going to the bar reception either. She preaches hell hot and holiness just like me."

"Well, tell your holy roller lady friend to take a hike. I am going to the reception and it is a relief that I won't be forced to sit with her."

"You are so disrespectful. My lady friend and I are praying that God bends and breaks Angela taking her health and whatever she loves the most till she calls on God for mercy. We are also praying that God strips you and puts you on your knees begging for mercy. You have enabled Angela for years. You share in every sin she has ever committed because you have bailed her out over and over hiring lawyers. You are on your way down, Mark. Taking Angela's gutter offspring is the first bend on your way to your knees."

"How can you be so cold and cruel to Angela and me?"

"I am not cruel or cold. Turning you over to God is an act of tough love."

"I will see you tomorrow mom. Do not bother introducing me to your lady friend. She sounds like a 'holier than thou' bitch to me." He replied mad.

"Watch your tongue, Mark. God hears everything you say and he doesn't think kindly of those speaking evil of his anointed. My lady friend is chosen and will be ordained as a minister."

"Right . . . goodbye mom."

CHAPTER SIXTEEN

Naomi Calls Home to Jack

It was early Sunday morning. Naomi had not been able to sleep because there was not a closet in her motel room big enough to make a pallet in and she was afraid. The worst part was, she did not know why she was afraid other than she had this recurring dream that the devil woman, she had met in the Nashville bus station two years before, was after her and those about her in some sort of small church with a knife. Ever since encountering the bus station Devil woman, she had been having night mares. In her sleep, the Devil woman would yell that Joel belonged to her. It was just a dream, but she knew that the woman was dangerous and she feared that the woman and Joel somehow followed her wherever she went. She couldn't explain her fear.

Naomi had told Rachael about the dream. Rachael agreed with her that she was being stalked by Satan. The two of them had said many prayers for God's protection.

Naomi rang Jack using a cell phone he had bought her before she left. He immediately answered.

"Good morning, Sweet Thing. I have been hoping you would call." He answered in a pleasant voice."Is the country air at Rachael's farm agreeing with you?" He had always thought that Rachael and her farm was part of Naomi's Amish settlement back in Missouri.

"I always find the air and the company of my friend agreeable. I arrived here safely yesterday afternoon. However, I am traveling with her for the weekend. She was invited to a wedding and I am accompanying her. We stayed in a motel room last night. It was exciting. I have never stayed in one before. How are you?" She inquired.

"A huge case I have been working on requires my attention today. I am driving as we speak to Nashville to coordinate the event. What is my Someday Girl up to?" He asked putting her on speaker mode.

"I am in a motel room in Nashville. When Rachael wakes up we will have morning prayers and then go have breakfast. I . . . I have no closet to sleep in. I slept in the bathroom where I could lock the door. The tile floor was very hard last night. I have not had a pleasant night."

"Tonight, if you have problems sleeping, imagine me with my arms around you. I will be with you in my thoughts and my prayers. I will imagine myself in yours because I had a rough night last night also. I stayed in a motel room in St. Louis last night. I had a little last minute of snooping to do. The guy in the room next to me snored so loud and so forcefully that he sounded like a freight train crossed with a buzz saw. Will you say a prayer for me that I sleep peacefully in a quiet motel tonight?"

Naomi snickered. "I will pray for you a peaceful room, if you will pray for my bathroom floor to turn into a fine mattress."

"I am missing you." Jack stated laughing. "Do you want me to come and rescue you from the tile floor and probably a very dull wedding?"

"I am looking forward to the wedding. I need a change of pace and something different to think about till my heart quits hurting and my divorce is final. If it makes you feel good, I am missing you more than you are missing me." She replied.

"That makes me feel good. You just keep on missing me till you just have to find your way back to me."

"I have a question I wish to ask you." She replied.

"What is it Sweet Thing? If you are asking me to be your man, the answer is that I have always been yours. You are my Sunday girl. The other six days, I have to share myself with the redhead and possibly a waitress or two." He stated laughing and teasing her.

"Oh you . . ." She replied snickering. "At least you are up-front with me about your Monday thru Saturday girls. I am glad that I am your Sunday girl. The other six will only bring you heartache."

Jack laughed. "Seriously, Naomi, why have you called? I can tell from your voice that you are antsy."

"I have a serious question to ask you. It is of a religious nature."

"What? You are asking me a question about religion? I haven't exactly been a regular in church or in reading the good book, Naomi. I never prayed till last winter when you taught me how. You are the educated one when it comes to God, not me."

"I am sure that you can answer this one." She replied confidently. "Do you think it is okay for women such as me to preach? In my Amish world, the answer is no. The women do not sit with the men, nor do they participate in service. Do you think God calls women like me to preach? I am considering laying down part of my Amish teachings. I would like to dedicate my life to helping others in the English world to find their God. You are the only family I have. I want an honest opinion from you. Is it okay for me to pursue a career as a lady minister?"

"Well, Sweet Thing, every human in society has a niche to fill, a place to display their special talents. If being a lady minister is your talent and calling, then I am going to have to work on straitening up my act because I would do nothing less as your family than sit on your front pew and support you. I would feel quite privileged to sit at your feet and listen just as the multitudes sat at Jesus' feet. I will be a follower of you and thankful for the opportunity." He replied.

"As a man, you would not see me as a threat because I would be holding a man's position in the English and Amish world?"

"You have my permission to choose a vocation that is, normally in our society, filled by men. I support you and always will in whatever you choose to do or not do."

"I love you, Jack. You always make me feel good about myself and my decisions. I am going to become a minister! I have also come to the decision that some women like me are intended to be born ugly and not have children. Perhaps, I am to love other's children like Rachael does her Sunday school ones."

"Now, I am going to scold you. For starters, Naomi, I don't know who has made you feel that you are ugly as a woman. You are far from it. You are the most gorgeous woman that I have ever encountered. Abusive men, with problems of their own, try to make women feel that they are ugly or not desirable to any man but them. They are control freaks who want to put you down and keep you down. You are beautiful and any man including me and Marcus should be groveling at your feet just for a wrinkle from your pretty little nose. I do find your nose to my taste."

"Marcus has twice chosen someone other than me. He chose Jenkins and Karen. He stood me up Friday evening as though my plans to walk down by the river meant nothing to him. I must be ugly."

"Marcus has made bad choices and he is the ugly one for them. As far as children, the right man will come along and you are probably going to be constantly pregnant for the next twenty years. He will probably have to trade his four door gray compact car in and drive a mini bus to accommodate at least a dozen children."

"Thank you, Jack. Keep your four door, gray, compact car Amish clean and the passenger side empty. When my heart silences itself, it will be you that I come home to. When I sleep tonight, I will indeed imagine your arms of protection around me. You are my Sunday man!"

"I will be waiting for you, Naomi. I need my Sunday girl in my kitchen."

"Well, you tell the Monday thru Saturday girls they had better not mess up that kitchen and leave it for me to clean up on Sunday morning. I do have a reputation for being a teeny bit violent."

Jack snorted and then laughed. "I love you, Naomi. Don't forget where home is."

"I love you too, Jack. When my heart has silenced itself concerning Marcus and my divorce is over, I will come home to you. It is you that has stood beside me."

"I will be waiting for you." He replied.

In the invisible, Frankie Frances turned to Osceola after listening in on Naomi's conversation.

"That two bit detective is blindsiding Marcus. It is Marcus that God has prepared for Naomi."Frankie Frances stated in her know it all, honey dipped voice.

"Marcus was indeed the one that the White Suit chose to pair Naomi up with. However, he is not Naomi's soul mate! Joel was. When a man abuses a gift given him, God takes the gift back and gives it to another. She was the gift and God took her back from Joel. He then gave a special gift to Naomi, because she no longer had a soul mate. He gave Naomi a traveling companion named Marcus."

"But doesn't Marcus have a soul mate somewhere, if Naomi isn't his?"

"Marcus has never been granted a soul mate because he has never embraced the light of God. Even as a child he turned from his mother's ministry and teachings. Soul mates are a reward for those following God."

"But how could God give Marcus to Naomi if he is a dark soul?" Frankie Frances asked looking confused with her glasses sliding down to the end of her nose.

"His mother is a child of God and she has interceded for her son asking that he turn from his evil ways. Naomi is the pivotal point for him. She is Marcus' chance to turn from his darkness, the answer to his mother's prayers."

"But Joel always returns to Naomi. Won't he show up again one day?"

Joel quit following God the first time he walked away from his farm and embraced a woman of the world. He will never return to the farm or Naomi. He has made his choice. Naomi is like Job in the Bible. He was stripped of everything he owned including his wife, children, cattle and land by Satan. God gave back to Job everything he had lost. Naomi has lost her husband, children, religious roots, respect, and all her worldly possessions other than what she could carry when she walked away. God is now in the process of giving back to her abundantly more than she lost. That includes a replacement for Joel."

"How about her two dead children, she does not wish replacements for them?"

"One day her heart will sing again and she will stand in the light of God putting aside her grief. At that point, she will be given more children. She will be paired either with Marcus or whomever God chooses for her to be with.

Joel has forever lost his soul mate. In my thinking, the White Suit is probably going to pair her with Jack."

"Jack has never been married or found his soul-mate. He cannot be God's gift to Naomi." Frankie Frances stated in her honey dipped southern young voice. Of the two men in Naomi's life, she preferred Marcus because he was the handsome one of the two. However, in her thinking, Corky Cameron was the best looking of all of them. He made her heart race.

"Jack is like Marcus. He has never walked in the light of God till he met Naomi. Unlike Marcus, he has slowly turned. Before meeting Naomi, he was not a candidate to be presented with a soul mate. Naomi has pointed him to the light and he has embraced it. He has not been granted a soul mate, yet. What God has given him is a love for Naomi and arms to protect her and provide for her. He is a replacement for Marcus in my thinking, a second traveling companion." Osceola Black Lightning stated pulling out her nail file to work on her nails. "I hope God gives us a chance to have our nails done before we tackle our next white cap mission. I've been wearing this same nail polish for over a year now."

"This is Nashville! We could probably find a good nail salon here." Frankie Frances stated looking at her own teen, baby pink, polished nails. "What color do you think Cory would like to see on a woman's nails?"

"On a woman's he would like to see a sharp color of red. However, you are still baby buggy material. You will not be wearing any color but baby girl pink till I say so. You are in my charge." Osceola stated in her syrupy, sticky, fly swatting southern voice.

"You just called me a baby. I am not baby buggy material, Ms. Osceola black Lightning. I am a woman in love and I just know that Corky Cameron is my soul mate. You can prevent me from red nails, but you can't stop me from loving him."

"Well, pink nails, you might just be a little shocked on our next adventure. You are going to have a little competition. I predict he develops a crush on a girl named Sarah. I think I recall your name being Frankie Frances." Osceola stated once more swatting her with her words.

"You are mean . . . Ms. Osceola Black Lighting. You are jealous because I am young and beautiful and you are an over the hill, obese piece of angel crap who can't catch a man and keep him anymore. I believe your long legged Jack Rabbit has never tried to make his way to you. Does that tell you anything?" Frankie Frances retorted in her honey dipped young voice.

"Well, does this tell you anything?" Osceola Black Lightning replied giving her nail file a little swish and letting a portal open with the two of them having a look at an Amish girl named Sarah who was quite beautiful. "Once he falls in love with her, you don't stand one chance in seven million of him ever noticing you or making his way to you. Now, leave my long legged Jack Rabbit out of this. He is waiting for me. Your current heart throb, named Corky, will not be." Then the viewing portal closed.

Frankie Frances began to cry and the skies opened up in Nashville and a torrential rain fell. When a mad angel cries, look out. The weekend in Nashville was not going to be a pretty one. Stormy weather was brewing and a tornado named Frankie Frances was in a havoc mode.

~   ~   ~

Does Naomi make her way back home to Jack or does Marcus find forgiveness in her arms? What about Frankie Frances? Does she earn her guardian angel status and snag Corky Cameron for a boyfriend, or does Sarah, Joel's cousin, end up with Corky? Does Osceola rid herself of her mouthy assistant? What about Naomi, does she get justice for her dead children? Does Joel pay for his life as a polygamist, or does he escape and disappear? Does James, Joel's brother, show up to claim Naomi's love? What about Martha Toombs? Does Abraham stick by her when she pulls her last dark deed and then goes crazy? Does Karen find out she is actually her husband Joey's half sister? More disaster is yet to come.

Read Black Lightning Series, Book 3, The Caged Wife.

Also by Jo Hammers

Black Lightning Series, Book 3, The Caged Wife

Black Lightning Series, Book 4, The Amish Witch's Quilt

Black Lightning Series, Book 5, The Night Traveler

Black Lightning Series, Book 6, Coffins and Cadavers

Black Lightning Series, Book 7, Ribbons of Darkness

Black Lightning Series, Book 8, Zook's Place

ORDER THIS SERIES FROM

www.paranormalcrossroads.com

www.ingramcontent.com/pod-product-compliance
Lightning Source LLC
Chambersburg PA
CBHW060816120626

46557CB00001B/240